### "Daniel, what are you saying?" Ruby asked carefully.

"I'm saying don't go back. I'm saying stay and start a *familye* with me, plan a future with me, bake cakes with me. I love you, Ruby King, and I plan on spending the rest of my life proving to you just how much."

The question caught her off guard. The declaration made her gasp. Ruby shook her head slowly. "It's only been a few months…"

Jacob had courted her for years and suddenly all of this was happening too fast.

"I found my happiness when I lost my heart to you. I only needed a minute to know that." Daniel reached for her hand. "I know it's fast, I know it's sudden, but I also know this is right."

Ruby cleared her throat, unable to form any words. She took a deep cleansing breath. Suddenly everything about Jacob came rushing back. Their courtship, their friendship, the breakup that tore her heart to pieces. Was she really ready to go through all that again?

**Hannah Schrock** is the bestselling author of numerous Amish romance and Amish mystery books.

# RUBY'S REGRET

## *Hannah Schrock*

ISBN-13: 978-1-335-92161-1

Ruby's Regret

First published in 2019 by Burton Crown Ltd.
This edition published in 2021.

Recycling programs
for this product may
not exist in your area.

This edition published by arrangement with Harlequin Books S.A.

For questions and comments about the quality of this book, please contact us
at CustomerService@Harlequin.com.

Harlequin Enterprises ULC
22 Adelaide St. West, 40th Floor
Toronto, Ontario M5H 4E3, Canada
www.Harlequin.com

Printed in U.S.A.

# RUBY'S REGRET

# Prologue

As with most love stories, this begins with three childhood friends. Ruby, Mary and Jacob.

Ruby and Mary King are sisters. Only two years apart in age, Mary is the youngest. Of course their mother dreamed her daughters would be inseparable, best of friends, which was true if you included Jacob Schrock.

Ever since they were old enough to understand the meaning of friendship, Mary and Ruby spent every free moment together. Their days were filled with chores, laughter and games.

As the years moved on, they each developed their own personalities.

Ruby King had a soft disposition, a generous heart and a kind smile. Although she did not possess the striking beauty of her sister, her auburn hair and forest-green eyes caught the attention of many boys her age. Ruby was humble and had no idea of the interest so many boys had in her. She likewise didn't realize Jacob's interest in her.

Mary King, the beauty of the King family, had sky-blue eyes and intricately braided blonde locks. Although her beauty was breathtaking it couldn't seem to hide her jealous nature. Mary always believed that she was not as blessed as everyone else. Her negative thoughts and angry nature sullied her breathtaking beauty, rather deterring interest than garnering it.

Jacob Schrock was as attractive as any young man could be, with jet-black hair and warm brown eyes. His mischievous smile won over the hearts of many young girls, but Jacob only had eyes for one.

Mary had dreamed of princes and princesses since the first time she read a story about "happily ever afters" at school. In her mind her happily ever after would come in the form of Jacob Schrock. In her heart she believed that one day Jacob would turn to her with more than just a friendly smile. He would turn to her with a knowing look, making it clear that his feelings for her had moved from friendship to love.

Mary lived by these dreams. Whenever Jacob was near, she dreamed of their future together. It dominated her every thought, every chore, every moment of every day. Mary was certain that in a few years she would stand in front of their congregation with Jacob at her side.

When she was twelve, Ruby's mother called her into the kitchen one afternoon, elated to share the news that Jacob's mother had agreed that the two were promised to be married. Ruby was surprised but excited by the news. She had always believed that her sister would be matched first but she couldn't be more pleased that she had been matched with her best friend.

Mary didn't respond when Ruby told her the news. It was supposed to be her; her mother had just handed her dream to Ruby. She didn't fight against it, she didn't bother going to her mother because that would be disrespectful, but she had been heartbroken.

After that day things slowly began to change. Mary's jealous nature seemed to increase and Jacob and Ruby only had eyes for each other. At first the small things affected her, like Jacob and Ruby running off without her, but the issues later became more obvious. They would arrange to meet by the stream without inviting Mary. Mary usually found them but ignored their disappointed expressions when she joined them.

She knew it wasn't what her parents wanted, but she wanted Jacob to see her. Matching Ruby and Jacob was a mistake and Mary needed everyone to realize this.

But no one did.

Ruby and Jacob began dreaming their own dreams. By the age of fourteen their relationship began to change. The changes imperceptible at first until they began dreaming of their future together. Ruby and Jacob's futures were aligned, their childhood friendship blessed with the promise of marriage. But Mary felt that she had been robbed of her future.

Ruby and Jacob still tried to include Mary in some of their activities but Mary slowly began to withdraw. She couldn't stand by and watch them fall in love.

As their relationship grew with every passing season, Mary's unhappiness amplified.

Although she was careful not to show her jealousy, Mary felt thwarted. She was prettier than Ruby and had liked Jacob forever, but it seemed both Ruby and Jacob were blind to her feelings, which only exacerbated them.

After their rumspringa they were all baptized into

the community. With baptism came Sunday singings. What Mary had only dreamed of now became a weekly reminder that she would never get to marry the boy of her happily-ever-afters.

At every singing Jacob and Ruby only had time for each other. They would ride in Jacob's buggy late into the night, angering Mary even more. Of course a few boys asked Mary to ride with them but she refused. Her heart was meant for Jacob and she wasn't about to share it. Her parents introduced her to young men eager to be matched, but Mary made it clear that she wasn't interested.

Her parents became worried, believing their daughter would rather be a spinster than a wife and mother; they had no idea about the unhappiness dominating Mary's heart.

Over time they each focused on their own talents.

Jacob had incredible carpentry skills, just like his father. He soon joined his father's carpentry business and flourished under his father's guidance. Everyone knew that one day Jacob would take over the business, making him all the more eligible.

Ruby had never had a penchant for much. Her skills were few but when it came to baking, she was a magician. Her cakes were soon sought after by every family in the community. Birthdays, baptisms, and anniversaries were all celebrated with a cake from Ruby. Of course her generous nature didn't expect payment. A simple thank you was more than enough for the kind-hearted Ruby.

Mary had shown promise since the first time she picked up a needle and thread. That promise turned into a great skill. The quilts she made graced every bed in their home and were soon sought out by the local farm stalls.

That confused Mary even more; she had the skills needed to take care of a husband and a home. She could cook, clean, and even sew and yet it seemed Jacob had forgotten she even existed. She understood he was now courting her sister, but she felt left out and excluded.

She was no longer included in the picnics or trips to town; it was as if Jacob and Ruby had forgotten about her altogether. The jealousy in her heart began to turn into a devouring anger, robbing her of every small happiness in her life. All she could see was how she had been thwarted by her sister and her best friend.

# Chapter One

Ruby stood in the large farmhouse kitchen, looking out the window as she mixed the cake batter. There was nothing as soothing as watching the butter, eggs, flour and sugar blend until they created a velvety mixture.

The cake she was baking today was for Jacob's cousin Peter who was turning fourteen. Ruby had offered to bake the cake, not only because she liked baking, but because it was a favor to Jacob.

Ever since they were promised to each other at the age of twelve, Ruby had been looking forward to the day she would become Jacob's wife. A year older than Ruby, Jacob had been a gangly boy at the age of thirteen. Since then he had grown into his arms and legs. His shoulders had thickened with hard work. His once smooth skin now boasted the stubble of a man when he didn't shave for a day. His jet-black hair that had once been tousled by wind and play was now always neatly brushed beneath his wide brim hat.

The warm brown eyes that twinkled with mischief when they were children now looked at her with love. Everything was falling into place, just as Ruby had dreamed it would. She added a little more sugar for luck along with a small amount of lemon zest and continued stirring the mixture. The lemony scent filled the air, bringing a smile to Ruby's mouth.

Her mother was a great housekeeper; everything always in its place, clean and tidy. Whereas her sister, Mary, could make quilts that could intrigue even the best Amish seamstress. Ruby hadn't their talents but she could bake. She could bake like no one else and she enjoyed it more than anything in the world.

Especially her lemon cream double butter cake.

When she began experimenting with baking at the age of fourteen, Ruby had always worked from a recipe. But like a carpenter knows his wood and his tools, Ruby knew her ingredients. Soon she was playing around with recipes, adding a little of this and removing a little of that. Her recipes were now completely her own, each with its own secret little twist that Ruby liked to keep to herself.

It wasn't that she didn't want to share her recipes; it was simply because she one daydreamed of owning her own cake shop. When that day came she would need an edge that made her cakes different, better and even more delicious than the competition.

A giggle escaped her. It was a lovely spring morning in Lancaster County and instead of focusing on the batter she was making, she was dreaming of the future.

But how could she not when the future lay ahead of her with such wonderful promise. Not only would she be marrying the boy of her dreams, she would have the rest of her life to spend with him. They would have beautiful children, their own home, and their dreams would be the same, as they had been for years.

Although they had been courting for two years, since their baptisms, Ruby knew the time for the announcement of their engagement was drawing closer. Traditionally, wedding season was in autumn, which meant they would be announcing in summer.

Excitement rushed through Ruby at the thought of announcing her engagement. Once the engagement was announced they would begin hand delivering the invitations, she would begin planning the wedding day itself and, of course, her wedding dress.

The thought of a wedding dress sobered her excitement briefly. When she was a little girl, she and Mary had promised each other to be bridesmaids, but these last few months it was as if Mary wanted nothing to do with her. Whenever Ruby tried to talk to her sister it was as if Mary ignored her, making it clear she didn't care what Ruby had to say.

It hurt more than Ruby liked to admit, but there was nothing she could do about it. Numerous times she had asked Mary what troubled her, but Mary would just scoff and walk away.

Ruby knew there was no one better to sew her wedding dress than Mary, but she had a feeling Mary wouldn't be interested in helping. Sewing was not one of Ruby's talents. She was hopeful her mother would have mercy, take pity, and help her.

Ruby tested the texture of the batter. Pleased, she began dividing it into three cake pans. She had stoked the wood stove to make sure it was the right temperature to bake all three cakes before she even started with the batter. Once the batter was divided equally, Ruby slipped the tins into the oven and began clearing up.

She knew that in the time it took her to clean the

kitchen and prepare the icing, the cakes would be ready. Just as she was putting away the last mixing bowl, the rich lemony scent began to fill the air. A smile formed on her mouth as she moved towards the oven. She opened the door and just as she knew they would, all three tins were ready to be removed. There was no need to test them; she could smell they were ready.

Once the cakes were set on the cooling rack, Ruby checked the time. It was a little after two o'clock. More than enough time for the cake to cool and for Ruby to do the frosting before Jacob would collect it after work.

Her mother walked into the kitchen after spending most of the morning on laundry. She was a combination of Mary and Ruby. She had Mary's blue eyes but Ruby's auburn hair and generous smile. "That smells delicious, I hope you made extra. You know how much *Daed* loves your lemon sponge cake."

Ruby nodded with a smile as she poured them each a cup of tea. "Of course I made extra. *Daed* would never forgive me."

After covering the frosting, Ruby took a seat at the table with her mother. There was always time in their home for a quick chat. "Have you seen Mary this morning?"

Her mother shook her head. "*Nee.* She seemed a little out of sorts this morning. I think she went into town for more fabric. The farm stall in Strasburg sold all the quilts they had in stock. She's in a hurry to make more."

"That's very *gut*," Ruby smiled. Her sister, now 21, had made a name for herself with her quilting and her quilts were sought after by almost every farm stall in the area. "*Gott* truly blessed her with talent."

Her mother smiled and reached for Ruby's hand, "He

blessed you as well. You should really consider opening a shop or at least selling your cakes."

Ruby frowned. Although her dream was to open a cake shop, it felt wrong making money out of something she liked to do when she'd always given her baked goods away for free. "One day perhaps, but I can't charge our community for a cake. It's the neighborly thing to do."

Her mother laughed and squeezed her hand, "Ruby, flour, eggs, sugar, frosting and even wood aren't free. At least charge them for the cost of baking a cake."

Ruby sighed, knowing her mother was right. She couldn't keep baking out of the household pantry for the rest of her life. "I'll think about it."

"*Gut*. Besides, a baking business is a *gut* idea for a girl who's about to get married. It's something you can do at home, something you can do even once you have *kinners* running around."

Ruby laughed, no one knew how much she looked forward to being a mother and having a family as much as her own mother. It was merely a matter of time now before all her dreams came true.

## Chapter Two

Mary stood outside the kitchen door and couldn't help but overhear her mother and sister's conversation. Jealousy burned through her heart and although she knew it was a sin, she couldn't seem to get rid of it.

All their years of being friends with Jacob, it was Mary who believed she would be promised to Jacob. She had built her little dollhouses pretending to be Jacob's wife, pretending to be the mother to his children.

Seven years ago her mother had ruined that dream when she announced that Ruby was the one promised to Jacob. At first Mary had believed she would with time accept her sister's betrothal but as time moved on, it seemed she couldn't accept it.

The bishop had invited her to meet a young man visiting from Maine just last month and although he seemed enamored at first, that all changed when she invited him to dinner. One look at the kind Ruby and his interest in Mary vanished.

Worse still was that Ruby didn't even notice the way men looked at her, she was oblivious to any man but Jacob.

Mary's Jacob.

Those strong arms should protect and hold her, not her sister. Mary quickly brushed away the tears that slipped from her eyes. How many nights had she cried over Ruby and Jacob's betrothal? How many nights had she prayed for God to help Jacob realize that she was the one he was meant to be with?

But none of her prayers were answered. In fact, God seemed to be ignoring her, just like Jacob and Mary.

Instead of joining in afternoon tea with her sister and her mother, Mary turned and walked in the opposite direction. She needed to do something to make Jacob realize his mistake. She knew it was hopeless to beg Ruby to step back. Her sister was in love and nothing and no one would come in the way of her love for Jacob, but there were other ways.

Mary just had to find one that would work.

She rushed towards the barn and quickly climbed into the hayloft. What was once a place of horror stories and home to rats had become Mary's hideout. It was the one place she could think, the one place she wasn't interrupted, the one place that held no memories of the friendship she had shared with Ruby and Jacob as children.

When they began to play alone, Mary had found solace in having a place of her own. A place where no one would interrupt her, a place where she could clear her mind and make the decisions that needed to be made.

Like the decision that lay before her now.

Was she going to accept her sister's marriage to the man she loved or was she going to find a way to end their fairytale before it started?

It was easy. The decision was made even before

Mary contemplated it. She had sat around for six years hoping Jacob would notice her. For six years she had kept her distance and prayed for guidance.

God only helped those who chose to help themselves.

Mary stared out the large window, out over the meadows, and a plan began to form in her mind. She didn't have to do anything as drastic as seduce Jacob, not that her Amish morals would allow for that, after all.

She just needed to plant a seed. A seed that would grow and grow until it was too big to ignore. A seed that would make Jacob realize that he was courting the wrong sister. A seed that would ruin her sister's dreams and make hers come true.

A shadow of guilt flickered in her mind but she quickly pushed it away. It wasn't that she didn't wish her sister happiness, in fact she wished Ruby every happiness the world had to offer, just not with Jacob.

Why couldn't Ruby be interested in all the men their parents and the bishop kept bringing by? Why couldn't Ruby realize that she had her pick of all the available young men in Lancaster, whereas Mary only had her eye on one?

It was hard to know that your sister wasn't as pretty or as talented as you, and yet she overshadowed your every move. The only thing Ruby was good at was baking. She couldn't iron, clean, sew or cook like Mary could, and yet everyone was blinded by her one talent.

Mary shook her head as an idea began to form in her mind. It wasn't even as if she had never had the thought before, in fact she'd thought it many times, but she had never acted on it. Never before had Mary seen the need to act as she did now.

Jacob and Ruby were about to announce next season,

and it was already the end of spring. If she didn't act now, her entire future and dreams would be ruined. It was time Mary took her happiness into her own hands. It was time for Mary to decide whether she was going to be the sister left behind or the sister following her dreams.

The time had come for Mary to walk into the sunset with Jacob by her side. She was more certain of that than she had been of anything in her entire life.

She watched her mother and sister side by side in the kitchen through the window and wondered if her mother ever realized how she felt. Did her mother not know that she was the one who loved Jacob?

Mary quickly brushed away the tear that slipped over her cheek. She was done blaming, hiding and pretending none of this mattered.

It all mattered and she was going to make sure she ended it before Mary no longer mattered to anyone.

Again the guilt flushed through her but this time she didn't just ignore it, she reasoned with it. Why should she feel guilty for a loving a man who deserved more than her sister?

There was nothing to feel guilty about, because Mary was about to change everything.

# Chapter Three

Ruby was baking again, this time for the bishop's anniversary.

Mary had finished her morning chores and would continue working on her quilt when she returned from town. First she had an errand to run, an errand that couldn't wait.

After telling her mother that she needed to go into town for more thread, Mary readied the buggy and horse and set off on her way. No one knew Jacob's routine like Mary did; she often doubted that even Ruby did.

Mary knew that Tuesday mornings Jacob came into town to the hardware store to place their weekly order of lumber. She also knew that after he placed his lumber order, he stopped by the grocery store to pick up a few things, that's where she planned on meeting him.

She arrived in town a little after ten o'clock. Her heart raced as she secured the horse and buggy and rushed into the grocery store. When Jacob arrived she had to look surprised to see him. She picked up a basket and started wandering the aisles, placing a few items inside, all the while keeping an eye on the door.

When the bells jingled, her heart skipped a beat. She glanced at the door and saw his familiar smile as he greeted the proprietor. His square jaw and regal nose gave him an air of authority. His black hair was due for a cut; his plain outfit was the one he wore to church. He looked dapper, handsome and every bit as he did in her dreams. Mary moved towards the aisle he disappeared into and took a deep breath as she rounded the shelves.

It couldn't have worked better if she had planned it that way. Just as she rounded the shelves, so did Jacob. They bumped into each other, the items from her basket spilling onto the floor.

"Ach Mary, I'm so sorry. I should have looked where I was going. Let me help you," Jacob smiled warmly as he bent to pick up the items. "Can you forgive me?" His charming smile made her heart leap like it always did.

Mary quickly adjusted her expression to one of angst. "*Denke*, Jacob. Of course you're forgiven."

With a heavy sigh she turned and walked away, counting the seconds until she heard him call.

"Mary, wait!"

She turned, her expression sad and waited for him to approach her. "What is it, Jacob?"

"What's wrong? You seem out of sorts. I'm really sorry about bumping into you."

Mary shook her head with a sad smile, "It's not that."

"Then what is it? We've been friends forever; you know you can tell me anything."

Mary drew in a breath and held his gaze before she finally shook her head, "I shouldn't. Really, it will only cause sadness and anger. I don't want to get in the middle of this."

Jacob frowned, stepping closer, "Mary, what are you talking about? What can only cause sadness and anger?"

Mary set down the basket and folded her hands together. "I didn't want to bother you, Jacob. We've been friends for so long, I don't want to be the one to ruin your happiness, but there is something you should know."

"What should I know?" Jacob was clearly confused. He shook his head as his brow furrowed again. "Talk to me."

"Not here," Mary said quickly. "If you have time, we can go to the coffee shop. There are too many prying ears in here for our conversation to be private."

Jacob checked the time on his pocket watch, contemplating for a brief second before turning to her. "I've got time. *Kumm.*"

Before Mary could agree, he slipped his hand through the crook of her arm and led her out of the grocery store to the coffee shop next door. Mary's heart raced in her chest. It was the first time in years she was alone with Jacob. The first time in years he seemed concerned for her. She hadn't even gotten to the best part of her plan and already it was working like a charm.

After ordering two coffees, Jacob turned to her with a concerned look in his eyes. "Talk to me. You know you can tell me anything."

Mary sighed heavily and squeezed out a few tears until she finally met Jacob's gaze. "I hoped my eyes deceived me, honestly I did. But they didn't. I tried to ignore it, but I can't, Jacob. Just the other day I came into town to buy thread and a pack of needles, when I saw them. Ruby was standing on the corner by the barber shop talking to another *mann*."

"To who?" Jacob asked, confused.

"It was an *Englischer*. She'd told us that she'd gone to see you. Then I came into town and there she was talking and laughing with an *Englisch mann*."

"Surely it's a just a misunderstanding. Ruby would never do anything to hurt me. She loves me. We're announcing in a couple of months."

"I know," Mary sighed and stared into her cup for a long while before she finally met his gaze again. "I know I shouldn't have told you. I knew I should rather have kept it to myself, but I can't stand the thought of my *schweschder* breaking your heart. We used to be friends too, Jacob, and I can't stand the thought of my *schweschder* hurting my friend."

Jacob took a sip of his coffee and shook his head again. "Mary, Ruby is nothing if not loyal. She wouldn't betray me. I'm sure what you saw was just Ruby talking to a friend. Perhaps someone she baked a cake for. I honestly do not believe that Ruby would do anything to hurt me."

Mary's nerves began to sizzle and snap, realizing her plan wasn't working. She had to turn things up a notch if she wanted this to work. "I understand how much you care for her, Jacob. Do you not realize how hard this is for me? I believed she loved you, I believed I would be aunt to your *kinners*. When I saw that... I couldn't believe it either. But it was her, Jacob. When I asked her that night, she denied ever being in town. Do you honestly think I'll mistake another person for my own flesh and blood?"

Jacob sighed, shaking his head, "*Nee*, I don't. I just can't believe it. I'm sure there must be an explanation. I'll ask her…"

"Are you going to ask her about the kiss as well?" The words were out before Mary could stop them. Not for one moment did she plan on lying about Ruby kissing another boy, but she was already in too deep to stop now.

"What kiss?"

"The kiss she shared with the *Englischer* before she walked away. It was the kind of kiss you give someone you love…." Mary trailed off knowing that Jacob hadn't even had the pleasure of kissing her sister yet.

# *Chapter Four*

J acob's brows drew together even as he felt his heart constrict in his chest. He blinked a few times to focus on Mary and slowly shook his head from side to side. "It couldn't be...not my Ruby."

Mary nodded sympathetically, "I know, I thought the same. But it was her, Jacob. What bothers me is why she didn't break things off with you before she began dallying with an *Englischer*. If *Mamm* and *Daed* find out...they are going to be so disappointed."

Jacob nodded, "I can only imagine. This could get her shunned."

"I know. Ach Jacob, I feel so bad for being the one to tell you, but it's weighed on my mind all week. I've tried to forget it, but every time I see her I'm back in the buggy watching from across the road. I don't even know who he is. If I did, I would have told you so you could get some answers for yourself."

Jacob pushed the cold coffee away and pulled a bill out his pocket. "I need to go. *Denke* for being honest with me, Mary."

"Always. You're one my dearest friends, always have

been and always will be. You know I'm always here for you."

Jacob nodded. He couldn't imagine how hard it must have been for Mary to tell him what she just did. To see her own sister commit such an act must have weighed heavily on her heart. For a brief moment while Mary told him, Jacob had been certain Mary was lying. Why would his beautiful and kind Ruby do something like that to him?

But then why would her sister lie about something that would influence the reputation and standing of their whole family?

Mary wouldn't lie about something this important.

As he walked away from the coffee shop, he couldn't help but wish that Mary hadn't told him. If she hadn't, he would still be dreaming about his autumn wedding with Ruby, he would be dreaming of moving into the *dawdi haus* on his parents' property, and of sharing his life with Ruby.

But all that now seemed like a vivid dream, a dream that was only bright and vivid because it would never come true. Perhaps Ruby wasn't the person he had always believed her to be. Perhaps her sweet disposition and kind soul were merely a façade for the real Ruby.

The Ruby who would go behind Jacob's back, behind her parents' backs, to meet an *Englischer* in town. To kiss an *Englischer* in broad daylight on a street corner as if she hadn't any self respect. In all the years they had been courting, Jacob had only ever held her hand.

The entire situation confused him. If Ruby didn't love him, if she didn't want to be Amish, why did she return after rumspringa to be baptized? Suddenly everything began falling into place for Jacob. Like an evil puzzle, all the pieces fit together. Ruby had never liked chores or housework, her only real love was for baking. She didn't attend the quilting or jamming bees in the community and much rather stayed home to bake cakes.

He had always believed her shy and adorable for not having the talents of her sister and her mother, but now he couldn't help but wonder if it was because she never wanted to be an Amish wife. Why didn't she tell him how she felt? Why didn't she come to him and tell him that she was unhappy? That she had found some-one new.

Of course Jacob would have been devastated, but at least he would have known the truth. To build your life, your dreams on someone who could sneak around behind your back with an *Englischer*…it was the worst kind of betrayal.

After settling his bill at the hardware store for the week's lumber order, Jacob headed to his buggy. He drove the horse harder than usual, wanting to get home. Ruby might think she had him under her spell, that she was the one pulling the strings in their relationship, but Jacob was done being a puppet. He wouldn't let Ruby get away with her lies for another day. Not only had she shattered his heart with her lies, she had expected Mary to keep silent about them for her.

How could she deny what happened when Mary had seen her? Suddenly the girl he had loved since he was a boy was a mystery to him. It was as if he had believed sugar was sweet all his life only to find out it was bitter.

He arrived home a little after noon and knew he wouldn't be able to focus on anything if he didn't first do what needed to be done. He searched through the kitchen drawers until he finally found a clean sheet of paper and a pen. Jacob took a seat at the kitchen table and began penning the hardest letter he'd ever written.

*Ruby,*

*You have robbed me of my dreams. For years, my happiness was tied to yours, my future entwined with yours.*

*That ends today.*

*I will not become a puppet in your puppet show. I have cut the strings and no longer have any ties to you. Under no circumstances can I go through with the wedding our parents have planned for years. If you need an explanation, look to yourself. I have changed my mind and hope that you will accept it as such.*

*Our courtship, friendship and engagement ends with this letter. Please do not try to contact me.*

*I wish you all the happiness you deserve, as long as it is not with me.*

*May Gott forgive you and help you find your way back to the girl you once were.*

*Regards,*
*Jacob Schrock*

Jacob read the letter over a few times. The words were hard; the strokes of the pen rough but it clearly portrayed the way he felt. He considered delivering it by hand but decided against it. He would ask one of his friends to deliver it to the King mailbox. Under no circumstance did he want to see Ruby King again.

For years she had captured his heart, dominated his dreams, and without warning she had ripped it all away. Their friendship, Jacob's trust and even her sister's loyalty. Jacob did not know who the real Ruby was, but he did know it wasn't someone he wanted to waste another minute of his time with.

If she could sneak around behind his back with an *Englischer*, then she was no longer the Ruby King he had fallen in love with as a teenager. She lost her way from God's path and although Jacob loved her more than life itself, he wasn't going to try and coax her back. For the first time in years, Jacob needed to focus on himself and his own life. He couldn't spend more time on a woman who didn't love him the way he had loved her.

He bit back the burning sensation in his throat. He wouldn't cry for her because he was certain Ruby didn't cry when she kissed that *Englischer*. He was also certain she didn't cry when she thought Jacob was too dumb to find out about it.

# Chapter Five

Mary couldn't believe how wonderfully her plan had worked. She had expected Jacob to confront Ruby, which would have led to an argument. She knew her sister well enough to know that she didn't like to be doubted. But it didn't even lead that far.

No, the day after she had met with Jacob, a letter had arrived at their home devastating Ruby's dreams and disappointing her parents. There had been tears but mostly there had been confusion. No one knew why the engagement had been ended, and what was worse, Jacob was not talking.

Mary had gone to Jacob's hoping to console him, but he had been so upset he had turned her away. Mary didn't let that scare her off; she knew it was only a matter of time before Jacob realized they were made for each other. She would give him a week before she made it clear to him that he had been courting the wrong sister all along.

Two days later Ruby hadn't yet joined them for dinner. It broke her heart to see her sister sad, knowing it was her doing; but in the long run, she had only done

Ruby a favor. Her mother had made them a lovely bean stew and the aroma wafted through the kitchen as they sat down for dinner.

Once they were all served, they said their silent prayers.

"Is Ruby not joining us for dinner?" her father asked after a short while.

Her mother sighed, shaking her head, "She's not eating. I can barely get her to drink tea during the day. This thing with Jacob doesn't sit right with me. He won't talk to me. I went by their place today and he refused to see me. That isn't like Jacob at all."

Mary fiddled with her plate, "It's between Jacob and Ruby, maybe you shouldn't try to interfere."

Her mother clucked her tongue. "Ruby is my *dochder* and when she's heartbroken to the point of starving herself, I will interfere."

"Exactly," her father agreed. "I went by the bishop today. Even he tried to find out what happened, but Jacob refused to speak to him. Apparently Jacob reminded him that courting was to be done in secret and that extended to breakups as well."

A heavy silence settled over the table. Mary glanced at her parents and saw the worry in their eyes. She quickly reminded herself that all of this would pass. She was just making sure that a horrible mistake wasn't made. Because if Jacob had married Ruby, that was exactly what would have happened.

Three farms over, Jacob sat in his room. He glanced out the window at the stars that shone in the night sky. It had been two days since writing the letter that ended his engagement to Ruby and he didn't feel better. He felt betrayed, and he felt ashamed for being the fool who had been betrayed.

What kind of man didn't know when his fiancée wasn't happy? What kind of man didn't know she was sneaking around behind his back? No kind of man at all, he reasoned.

Perhaps he wasn't ready for marriage. Perhaps he wasn't ready to be a husband and a father, when he couldn't even keep track of his fiancée. The shame and heartache dominated his every breath. He kept remembering a time when he and Ruby had been inseparable. When her laughter could have brightened the darkest day, a time when he was certain of her love and devotion.

He remembered the conversation with Mary and couldn't help but imagine how hard it must have been for her. Ruby was her sister, her baby sister, her only sister. How much it must have hurt Mary to tell him about Ruby's betrayal.

The more he thought about it, the angrier he became. He couldn't fathom why Ruby hadn't just told him she wasn't interested. Why couldn't she have been honest and come clean about her feelings rather than betraying him?

When Mary had come to see him, Jacob had known it was rude to turn her away. She was simply concerned. But Jacob didn't want Mary's concern. He couldn't help but blame her just a little for telling him the truth. In his heart he knew the truth mattered more than living a lie, but it would take a while for him to be able to face Mary again. At least until he knew how to support her, after all she was suffering as well with the heavy weight of her sister's betrayal.

His parents kept asking him what happened but he refused to tell them about his weakness as a man. When David King, Ruby's father had come to see him, he couldn't face the man that would have become his father in law. David was a like a second father to him. How could he tell David that Ruby was seeing an *Englischer*? He couldn't stand the thought of seeing the disappointment in David's eyes.

Today the bishop had come knocking and Jacob had done all he could to avoid the conversation. Never in his life had he been disrespectful to the bishop. Never had he even considered turning the bishop away, but how could he seal Ruby's fate, to cause her to be shunned by sharing her dark secrets? Even if she didn't love him, he still loved her. He wouldn't be the person responsible for her shunning.

He had spoken to the bishop about the tradition of courting. He had explained how courting had become a common affair in their community where it once was a private and sacred institution. No one knew of a courtship until the day a courting couple announced. He reminded the bishop of the way it should be done and had shied away from the truth long enough for the bishop to realize he wasn't going to divulge the reason for the break up.

Jacob had envisioned his future with Ruby, he had dreamed of a home and children, with Ruby at the helm of the house. Now his dreams were bleak, void of any happiness.

If he couldn't make the one girl happy whom he had loved for years, how could he ever make another happy? How could he be a father and a husband, if he couldn't even control his childhood love?

No, he reasoned, control was the wrong word. He had never wanted to control Ruby any more than he wanted her to control him. He simply wanted her faithfulness and her loyalty; she didn't even give him that.

A heavy sigh escaped him as he slipped beneath the covers. He closed his eyes and waited for sleep to numb his aching heart. That was the only place he found solace at this stage, everything and everyone else reminded him of what he had lost.

## Chapter Six

A week after receiving the letter that shattered her heart, Ruby was no closer to getting answers. She had considered going to see Jacob herself but the words in his letter had seemed so angry, so disappointed, that she couldn't stand the thought of seeing that in his eyes.

She kept to herself and spent most of the time in her room trying to find the answers for herself. She read Jacob's letter over and over again and couldn't fathom why he would say such things. Their relationship had been flawless, a miracle from God, she had always thought. And yet he had broken up with her without even facing her.

In the past week, she couldn't help but wonder if she had misjudged Jacob all along. Surely, if he loved her, he would've come to her if he had questions or concerns. Instead he wrote her a letter, ending a lifelong friendship and a two year courtship with a few words on paper.

Ruby knew she couldn't starve herself forever, especially since she could feel her clothes begin to sag. She helped her mother with chores, but didn't take part in the usual conversation they shared. Ruby knew her mother was trying to ease the pain, but nothing could ease the pain.

She had overheard her father mention that both he and the bishop had gone to see Jacob. Neither had managed to get the answers Ruby so desperately wanted. It was as if she had closed her eyes for a split second only to open them to find her world fallen apart.

Ruby kept glancing at the clock on the wall, waiting for the day to pass. Last night Mary had been kind enough to offer to talk to Jacob. Ruby wasn't sure her sister would manage any better than her father or the bishop had, but it was her last chance at understanding why Jacob ended their engagement.

Her parents also believed the plan worthy and begged Mary to see if she could get them any answers. Mary had left for Jacob's over an hour ago and was due to return any moment. In her heart she knew that Mary couldn't get Jacob to reconcile their relationship but at least she hoped to understand why their relationship was irreconcilable in the first place.

"Stop, she'll get back when she gets back," her mother said kindly when Ruby looked out the window again.

She nodded and tended to the chore at hand, scrubbing floors. The hardwood floor had been laid by her great grandfather more than a century before. Even though the wood had been cared for over the years by her family, it loved to gather dust and grime, and nothing cleaned it like a good scrubbing once a month.

It was a chore everyone hated, but one that needed to be done.

When Ruby heard the horse hooves nearing the barn,

her heart jumped into her throat. She kept scrubbing until Mary walked into the kitchen.

"And?" her mother asked before she could. "What does he have to say for himself?"

Mary shook her head, defeated. Ruby didn't have to hear the words to know her sister's answer.

At that moment her father came in from the barn as well. "Did you see Jacob?"

Mary nodded. "*Jah*, he spoke to me." Mary moved to the basin and poured a glass of water. Ruby watched as her sister drank down the entire glass of water before she turned and took a deep breath. "Jacob asked me to speak on his behalf. I know this must be hard for you, Ruby, but at least he spoke to someone."

Ruby nodded, unable to understand why her fiancé would choose her older sister as a mouthpiece. She pushed the thought away and listened eagerly.

"What did he say?" David urged his eldest daughter.

"He said that he meant what he said in the letter. He changed his mind. It was a betrothal orchestrated by both of your parents and he wasn't willing to be party to those arrangements anymore. He also mentioned something about being tired of being a puppet with someone else pulling the strings?" Mary shook her head as if baffled by her own words.

Ruby felt her cheeks warm with embarrassment. That was the one part of the letter she didn't understand at all. She had never told Jacob what to do, she had never even asked him to do anything she knew he wouldn't want to do. How was she pulling the strings?

"Anything else?" Ruby turned as her mother asked.

"*Nee*. Only that he wishes for everyone to leave him

alone so that he can go on with his life. And for Ruby to go on with her life as well."

Ruby nodded slowly. Her sister had said nothing that she hadn't read in the letter. If anything, she was more confused than before. She loved Jacob with all her heart and couldn't understand why he felt this way.

It was as if the more she tried to understand his decision, the more she was confused by it. Before he had sent the letter they hadn't disagreed for months. They barely ever argued. In fact they'd never had a fight in their lives.

Something must have happened to make Jacob change his mind, but Ruby couldn't understand what it was. She found her whole family looking at her with a questioning gaze and simply couldn't take it for another second.

Ruby turned and ran out the kitchen door as fast as her legs could carry her. She rushed past the barn, past the outhouse and into the meadow until her legs ached before she finally collapsed on her knees.

Tears streamed down her cheeks as she rested her hands on her thighs fighting for her breath. She knew that you prayed when you were calm and when you could bask in the glory of God's presence, but she needed Him now.

"*Gott*, why? Please help me understand why. I have done nothing to wrong Jacob. I have loved him for so many years; I can't imagine my life, my future, without him. I know You have a reason for all things, *Gott*, but what could be the reason for taking him from me? I love him, I love him more than I have ever loved and now it seems that not even that was enough? *Gott*, please help me, help me get rid of this gaping hole where my heart used to be. Help me heal and take away this sadness. I need You now, *Gott*, more than ever before. You have given me so many blessings, *Gott*, the biggest one of them Jacob. I know there is reason in taking him away from me, but please just tell me why. I can't go on without knowing what I have done to make him turn against me. Help me, *Gott*, help me find the reason and find a way to move forward without him."

As she finished her prayer, a butterfly flitted over the tall grass and landed on her hand. Ruby wasn't a fanciful person but in her mind it was God's way of telling her that everything would be alright. Even the darkest of nights is followed by a sunrise in the morning. Ruby just had to hang until dawn broke through the darkness that dominated her heart.

## Chapter Seven

David King couldn't stand seeing his youngest daughter heartbroken. He would have thought that after three weeks she would have been her old self again but instead, it seemed as time moved on, the more depressed she became.

He tried talking to Jacob again, but once again Jacob refused to see him. After Mary's declaration that Jacob stood by his decision, anger had replaced his confusion. Ruby was a wonderful girl and Jacob would be lucky to have her as his wife. He couldn't fathom why Jacob would end an arrangement that had been made years ago. What could Ruby have done to deserve this cold treatment?

The one day Ruby had been blissfully in love, even talking about the color of dress she wanted for the wedding, and the next the letter from Jacob had arrived. David wasn't a violent man, never had been, but seeing his little girl heartbroken and confused brought out the anger in him. He wanted to do something to ease her pain but he knew he was helpless against another man's decision.

After spending most of the day in the fields, he arrived home only to find Ruby isolated in her room again. Mary was helping her mother with dinner and chatting amicably, while Ruby once again refused to spend time with her family.

David walked to her room after washing his hands. "Ruby, come join us for dinner."

"I'm not hungry," came her sullen reply as she sat on her bed staring out the window.

David clenched his fists at his side. "Ruby, please. We're worried about you. You're becoming as thin as a scarecrow. Please join us."

Ruby turned around and it pained David to see the hollows in her cheeks, the shadows beneath her eyes and the lost look in her gaze. "I'll be there shortly."

She turned back to the window and for the first time since Jacob's letter arrived, David knew she couldn't stay here. She needed to get away from the sympathetic looks, from the community that had known about the engagement and now knew that his daughter was no longer good enough for Jacob Schrock.

Ruby joined them for dinner. David watched as she picked at her plate, only five bites made it to her mouth before she thanked Anna for the meal. Without asking her, she cleaned the kitchen before retiring to her room.

David waited until Mary excused herself to wash before he turned to Anna, "We cannot let her go on like this."

His wife sighed heavily. "Don't you think I know this? Don't you think I know that she's hurting, that every single time she sets her foot out the door someone is wondering why Jacob broke off the engagement? I just don't know what to do about it."

David nodded as he reached for his wife's hand. "I know. I also know that staying here is only going to make it harder on her. Do you remember your cousin we went to visit after our wedding?"

"Elizabeth?" Anna asked surprised. "What about her?"

"You once mentioned that she and her husband were never blessed with *kinner*s?"

"*Jah*, they weren't blessed like us, David. Her husband passed away the year before last. Do you remember, we couldn't attend the funeral?"

"*Jah.*" David nodded. "I know Ruby has never met her, but I think it would be *gut* for Ruby to go and visit."

"What? In Ohio?" Anna asked, surprised. "Why would you want to send her way? Hasn't she been punished enough?"

David shook his head patiently as he squeezed his wife's hand. "Not as punishment, Anna, as a reprieve. I think it will be easier for her to work through her emotions and her sadness when she isn't faced with everyone's sympathies whenever she walks out the door. I've given this quite some thought and I think it's the only way she can move past this. She's not eating, she's not going to town, all she does is sit in her room."

Anna sighed heavily. "She's not even baking."

David's heart clenched at the news. "I know Ohio is a long way from home but it will only be for a few months. I'm sure your cousin would welcome her coming now that she's a widow. We'll ask Ruby to go because her aunt is lonely. Even lost in her own pain, she'll always put another's needs before her own."

Anna debated on the thought for a while before she finally nodded. "David King, you don't often have *gut* ideas, but I think this one makes up for all the bad ones. I want to help her, I want to be there for her, but you're right. Being here is making things harder for her than it should be. I'll write to Elizabeth and explain the situation."

"*Gut*. But don't write, Anna; see if you can reach her by phone tomorrow. They ought to have phone shanties in Ohio."

"They do. Hopefully by tomorrow night we'll have an answer."

David watched as a tear slipped over his wife's cheek. "I know this is the right thing to do but I'm going to miss her so much."

"It will only be for a few months. Just until she's ready to face everyone here again."

"*Jah*, you're right. I'm sure Elizabeth will be happy to have her. Especially if she starts baking again."

"She will. She's nursing a broken heart and I'm the first to admit I didn't realize how strong her feelings were for Jacob. I think I believed they just liked each other because they were betrothed. Now I realize that she truly loved him. For him to stomp on her heart like that…"

"David, we can protect our *dochders* from many things in this world, but not from heartbreak," Anna said with an encouraging smile.

"I know. *Kumm*, let's head to bed." David stood up and smiled lovingly at his wife. He wanted that for his daughters. Their marriage had been arranged and David had fought tooth and nail against marrying the girl from Ohio. But his parents insisted they needed new blood in the community. When she had arrived on the bus, everyone in town talked about the beauty from Ohio, but David wasn't interested.

He wanted to find a partner on his own. He wanted to choose who he was going to spend the rest of his life with. Until he met her on their wedding day.

It wasn't her beauty or her pretty smile that made him fall in love, it was her eyes. Her eyes had drawn him in and made him see a future with her. At first their relationship was a little stilted, both a little intimidated by being caught in an arranged marriage, but it didn't take long for their awkwardness to thaw.

David wouldn't trade his wife for any other person in the world. Anna King was now his world. His prayers every night since his first daughter was born were that they would find the same kind of love he shared with Anna. He knew God had a plan for his daughters, he just wished that plan didn't include heartbreak.

## Chapter Eight

Ruby knew it wasn't punishment, it was a favor to her parents, but she still couldn't help but feel like the exiled child as she walked into Elizabeth Beiler's home. After the nine-hour bus trip all she wanted to do was sleep, but her mother's cousin couldn't seem to stop talking.

"So this is the kitchen," Elizabeth said over her shoulder with a broad smile. She was a little thicker in the waist than Ruby's mother, but her blue eyes were warm. Her hair was dark brown and her smile friendly as she gave Ruby a tour of the house. "This is my bedroom; this will be yours. I put on some fresh linen for you. Through here you have the living room. We had some modern plumbing put in just before my husband died, so the bathroom is through here. I usually get up just after five am to do the chores. I have chickens, the horses and of course the goats." Laughter bubbled from her throat. "Not many people like goats, but I simply adore them. I make goat's milk cheese and even have some young mothers who buy the milk for their *bopplin*."

Ruby nodded as she followed Elizabeth through the house until they finally returned to the kitchen.

"I know you must be tired after the long journey, so I already prepared dinner. I hope you don't mind chicken pie. Would you like some *kaffe*?"

Ruby couldn't help but smile at Elizabeth who seemed very excited about Ruby's visit. In her mind she had envisioned a bitter widow on the verge of a breakdown. Elizabeth was anything but. She was energetic, independent and seemed to love the idea of having her cousin's daughter come to visit.

"Chicken pie would be fine, *denke*." Ruby took a seat at the table as a cup of coffee was placed in front of her.

"I know the bus ride is terribly long. It wasn't too bad, was it? I know when your parents came to visit for their honeymoon, your mother complained about aches and pains for two days. But I guess back then the busses weren't as comfortable as today. Two helpings of mashed potatoes or one?" she paused just long enough for Ruby to answer before she continued. "Anyhow, they stayed with us for a week. I never thought Anna's daughter would come to visit me. It was such a surprise to hear you were coming."

Ruby nodded, wondering if her parents had told her about the broken engagement. "I was excited to come. I've never been away from Lancaster before."

"Well, interesting fact, Holmes County is the biggest Amish community in the USA. Did you know that?"

Ruby shook her head as a plate was set down in front of her. The rich aroma of chicken pie tingled the taste buds that had been numb for weeks. She couldn't remember the last time she was hungry. While Elizabeth continued to dole out facts about her community,

Ruby thought back to the conversation she had with her mother. Her mother had suggested she visit her widowed cousin for a month or two. Not only would Elizabeth have the company she so needed, it would give Ruby a chance to get over the heartbreak.

Ruby hadn't been very keen at first, until she remembered the sympathetic gazes everyone gave her. If her father urged her to smile or eat one more time, she wasn't sure she'd have remained cool and composed. She had her doubts about coming, especially since she wanted to heal her broken heart in her familiar territory; but perhaps the bubbly Elizabeth was exactly what she needed.

"The pie was made from fresh chicken this morning. I'll tell you I've been cooking and cleaning the whole day. Your mother tells me you bake?"

Suddenly caught off guard by the question, Ruby frowned. She hadn't baked since the day that Jacob broke up with her. For a moment she was lost in her own thoughts, wondering why the breakup had made her set aside the one thing that had always brought her joy.

"Or is that your *schweschder*? I must say, I have a tendency to listen with half an ear. I usually have my next question formulating even as I listen to someone else talk," Elizabeth laughed, and Ruby looked up with a smile. She was going to have to catch on to Elizabeth's strange Ohio Dutch accent quickly, since it seemed Elizabeth was a real chatterbox.

"It's me. I bake," Ruby said before taking a bite of the best chicken pie she had ever eaten in her life. The chicken was flavorsome and moist and the pie crust crispy but decadently buttery. She took another large bite, hoping Elizabeth didn't hear when her stomach growled.

"That's alright," Elizabeth laughed, making it clear she did hear. "I also forget to eat when I'm travelling." She gave Ruby an encouraging smile before she paid attention to her own plate.

Ruby smiled as she took a mouthful of the creamy mashed potato. She didn't tell Elizabeth that she had barely eaten for the last few weeks. She didn't know if it was the bus trip, the change in altitude or Elizabeth's cheerful company, but she was famished. She finished her plate of food and before she could ask, Elizabeth offered her more. "You're thin as a scarecrow, girl; a *mann* doesn't like to sleep with a stick." She laughed at her own joke as she dished up another healthy serving for Ruby.

"*Denke*," Ruby said before tucking in. Right now the last thing she wanted to think about was a man. When the bus had pulled out of town, she had glanced longingly in the direction of Jacob's home and wondered if he would even realize she was gone.

That, if anything, had made her realize that coming to Holmes County was the right thing to do. She needed to stop thinking about a man who had stolen her heart only to toss it back in her face. In Lancaster it had been hard to see through the sadness that dominated her days, but there was nothing like an eight-hour bus ride to make you see the trees for the forest.

As she put more distance between her and the man she loved, the anger slowly began seeping in. Why wouldn't Jacob talk to her directly? Why break up with her in a letter without even a proper explanation? If he truly loved her, surely he would have come to her when something bothered him? Instead, he had written a letter that had burned her dreams to ashes.

"You seem lost in your own thoughts. Is it about that boy?" Elizabeth asked without preamble.

There it was, Ruby realized. Her mother had told Elizabeth about her break up with Jacob. "*Nee*, I'm done wasting time over a boy who didn't really love me in the first place."

Elizabeth's brows drew together for a moment before a smile spread across her face. "When you meet the right *mann*, he's worth every second of your time, but the wrong one just wastes it. I say good riddance. The right one will come along, just you wait."

Ruby smiled although she doubted Elizabeth's words. After Jacob's treatment of her, she didn't think she ever wanted to fall in love again. If love was only heartbreak waiting to happen, she'd rather spend her time on more joyful activities like baking.

## Chapter Nine

Mary couldn't have planned it better herself. With Ruby moping around, it was hard to get Jacob to take notice of her. But now with Ruby away in Ohio, she had nothing and no one standing in her way.

She made sure to be in town whenever she knew Jacob would be there, to offer her support whenever she could. Jacob was still a little heartbroken himself, but that didn't deter her. With Ruby out of the picture, Jacob would soon forget her younger sister and realize that Mary was the one he should have been courting all along.

It was a mistake made by their parents years ago, one that Mary intended to rectify now.

Mary was grateful that Jacob hadn't spoken to anyone about what she told him. If he did, she might just find herself in hot water. Luckily for her, Jacob was more concerned with avoiding any connection to Ruby than seeking out the reason for her betrayal.

Even her parents were in better spirits since Ruby had left. She loved her sister and wanted her to be happy, but Mary couldn't help but realize how much better it was without Ruby. Her parents gave all their attention to Mary and praised her talents at quilting. Her favorite meals were made for supper, and around the dinner table she was asked how her day was.

Perhaps she should have been an only child, Mary wondered to herself as she thought about events of the last few weeks. Then she and Jacob would have been best friends, and they would have been betrothed.

Guilt briefly flickered in her mind but she pushed it away. She wouldn't feel guilty for seeking her own happiness, especially not when it was within her reach. She had loved Jacob ever since she was a little girl and it was only a matter of time before he forgot about Ruby and his feelings for her.

She missed Ruby every now and then but that she also pushed from her mind. The longer Ruby stayed in Ohio, the better it was for her plan to win over Jacob's heart.

It was late on a Thursday afternoon and the sun was shining through the window, dust mites dancing in the rays that shone inside. Jacob wiped the sweat from his brow as he worked. His father had gone to the bank and Jacob was all alone in their workshop.

Jacob couldn't help but regret not seeing Ruby before she left for Ohio. When Mary had told him about her sister's departure, he couldn't help but wonder if he should have spoken to Ruby instead of writing the letter. His heart was broken because of her betrayal, but he couldn't marry someone that could sneak around behind his back.

He had given Ruby every piece of his heart; he had loved her more than he had ever loved before. He had dreamed of their future together and yet she had tossed it all to the wind with an *Englischer*.

The only upside about Ruby leaving for Ohio was that now she couldn't be with her *Englisch mann* either. Was that why her parents had sent her away in the first place? With the thoughts rummaging through his mind, Jacob sanded the chest of drawers he was busy with. Ever since the breakup, he had spent almost every free minute working. Of course his father didn't complain about his sudden devotion to carpentry, but for Jacob it was a way of forgetting the girl he loved.

When the door to their work shed opened, Jacob kept sanding the chest of drawers. It was probably just his father returning from the bank. And then the man spoke.

"I think it's time you and I talked." The voice was deep and Jacob didn't need to look up to know it was David King.

"Mr. King," Jacob sighed. "I really don't have anything to talk about."

He hoped that the man would leave, that the man would spare him from the truth he knew about Ruby, but instead he walked towards Jacob. "You have a lot of explaining to do. My girl did nothing to you. For years she trailed after you like a love-sick puppy. We believed you loved her as well but clearly we were mistaken. If you really loved her you wouldn't have tossed her aside like a dirty rag without even an explanation." David's voice boomed through the shed and for the first time since he had penned that letter, Jacob found his own anger. He stood up and tossed the sandpaper aside before moving towards David.

"I did not toss her aside. She tossed me aside. After everything I did, after all the dreams we had for our future. She didn't even have the courage to tell me. I ended our relationship to save her the embarrassment." Jacob flinched, knowing he had already said too much. He didn't want to slander Ruby's name with her father, but he knew there was no backing out now as David's brow drew together in confusion.

"What in heavens are you talking about? What didn't she have the courage to tell you? What should Ruby have been embarrassed about? You're only making things worse than they already are. At least have the courage to tell me what you mean."

Jacob sighed and picked up a rag. He wiped his hands, shaking his head before finally meeting David's gaze. "Ruby was sneaking around with an *Englisch mann* behind my back. They kissed on Main Street in clear view of the whole community. How was I supposed to sit back and pretend I didn't know?"

David stumbled back a few steps, shaking his head. "*Nee*, that's ludicrous. My Ruby would never…she loved you. I saw the way she suffered after you broke up with her. That wasn't the suffering of a girl in love with another *mann*."

Jacob shrugged. It pained him to know he caused the anguish in David's eyes, but maybe it was better if David knew. Now he would stop bothering Jacob about giving him answers. "I know, but I couldn't go through with a wedding when my fiancée already went behind my back to see another *mann*. I hoped to spare her the embarrassment of you knowing. But now you know."

"*Nee*, I can't believe this, Jacob. Do you? Did you see it with your own eyes? Ruby is faithful and a loyal girl, she would have never…"

"I didn't see it, but I will say that my source is more

than reliable. I take my source's word as gospel, and even loyal and faithful girls can stray. I'm sorry, Mr. King, I know this must be hard on you but now you know why I didn't want to tell you."

David sighed heavily. "I still don't think your source is as loyal as you think, but I will ask you to keep this information to yourself. Anna doesn't have to know. Ruby is in Ohio and she won't return until this has all blown over. I'm asking you to let it blow over for the sake of my *dochder's* return."

Jacob nodded and watched David walk away without a parting greeting. The last thing he wanted was to tell David King that his daughter was having a fling with an *Englischer*, but hopefully now they understood. Hopefully now they realized sending Ruby to Ohio might have been the best decision for all of them.

## Chapter Ten

"My dear girl, if you continue baking like this you'll have to roll me alongside the buggy one of these days," Elizabeth wiped her mouth with a napkin. "Your mother said you could bake, she didn't say you were a magician with flour and eggs. These cakes are amazing."

Ruby laughed. A few days ago she had accompanied Elizabeth into town and bought all the ingredients she needed to bake. For the last few months, she hadn't so much as touched a mixing bowl but now it was like coming home again. When she started, she couldn't seem to stop. Over the last two days she had baked all her favorite cakes; the lemon butter cream, the double chocolate, coffee surprise, vanilla heaven and her famous carrot cake. Of course, between her and Elizabeth, there was no way they would be able to eat all the cakes.

"You should really give some of the cakes to your friends. I was having so much fun; I didn't even consider we won't be able to eat all of it." Ruby glanced at the five cakes standing on the kitchen table. All had only one or two slices missing.

"*Nee*. I'm not giving a single slice away unless you

come with me." Elizabeth got up and began taking down all her cake tins. "I have just enough tins for these cakes. While you place them in the tins, I'm going to ready old Hamlet and the buggy."

Before Ruby could disagree, Elizabeth disappeared out the back door. She had no idea where they were taking the cakes but at least they would be eaten. Ruby boxed all the cakes and carried them to the buggy one by one as Elizabeth hitched the buggy to the horse's harness. Hamlet, the large colt, sniffed at the tins as Ruby walked past him. "Where are we going?"

"To Fischer's," Elizabeth said before she climbed into the buggy and took the reins. "Is that all of them?"

Ruby nodded before confusion dawned in her eyes. "Fischer's? Is that a friend of yours?"

"*Nee,*" Elizabeth laughed, flicking the reins. "But they will be friends of yours pretty soon."

Completely baffled by Elizabeth's statement Ruby sat back and enjoyed the ride to town. She knew Elizabeth had something up her sleeve; she just had no idea what it was. In the two weeks since she arrived in Holmes County, Ruby had quickly learned that Elizabeth was just as bubbly as she was full of surprises.

Like the morning Ruby walked outside to find Elizabeth painting the barn. She didn't know what her mother thought about her cousin, but one thing was certain, Elizabeth had moved on after losing her husband. She grasped life with both hands, making the best of every day. Elizabeth's positive outlook and go-getter attitude made Ruby realize that a broken engagement wasn't the end of the world. She had lost her husband, the love of her life, and yet she didn't sit around moping about what could have been or what should have been, instead she lived life to the fullest.

They drove into the small town just a few miles from Elizabeth's home. The Main Street was teeming with Amish people. There were a few Amish stores in town including an Amish furniture shop. Ruby had only been to the grocery store and the post office since her arrival and didn't recognize the shop when Elizabeth stopped the buggy in front of an awning with "Fischer's" emblazoned on it.

Her brows drew together when she read the small wording beneath the name.

Amish Bakery.

"Elizabeth, what are we doing bringing cakes to a bakery?" Ruby asked a little apprehensively.

"You'll see." Elizabeth hopped out of the buggy with an energy reminiscent of a two-year-old. When Ruby didn't follow, she cocked her hands on her hips and raised her brow. "Ruby King, if you don't get out of that buggy, I'll bring the Fischers out to meet you."

Knowing she didn't really have a choice, Ruby jumped out of the buggy and followed Elizabeth into the bakery. The scent of chocolate, cream and custard met her as they stepped through the door. A woman on a mission, Elizabeth stepped up to the counter. "I'm looking for the owner."

A ghost of a smile played on the Amish man's face. His hair was brown, but more the shade of new bark than the dark shade of wet dirt. His eyes were bluer than the awning outside the door and amusement twinkled in them. "You're looking at him."

"*Gut*," Elizabeth turned and summoned Ruby closer.

"I'm Elizabeth Beiler and this here is Ruby King. Ruby is visiting us from Lancaster."

"It's a pleasure to meet you both." He smiled at Ruby and her heart skipped a beat.

"Now that formalities are out of the way, I'll tell you why we're here," Elizabeth steamrolled ahead. For a brief moment, Ruby wondered if Elizabeth ever gave someone else a choice when she set her mind on something. "I've bought a cake or two from you in the past and although I kept my opinions to myself, it's time I said something. The drudgery you call Amish baking is dry, crumbly and doesn't have a tenth of the taste of Ruby's cakes. Instead of wasting your time baking horrible cakes, you should buy Ruby's."

Ruby nearly swallowed her tongue. In one sentence, Elizabeth had just insulted the proprietor and made a business proposition Ruby had no idea about.

The man glanced from Elizabeth to Ruby and a smile slowly began to form on his mouth. "I'll be honest with you," he whispered. "I'm not fond of our cakes either. Ever since my *mamm* passed away, we've tried baking with her recipes but it's just not the same."

Ruby smiled, knowing the deceased woman probably had a few secrets to her recipes just like Ruby did.

"We couldn't stop baking cakes, but we focus on the fresh bread and pastries. Before I agree to outsource the baking side of my business, could we taste her cakes?" he directed the question at Elizabeth, but his smile was aimed at Ruby.

"I'll fetch them while you two get acquainted," Elizabeth said before heading to the buggy.

As soon as she was out of earshot, Ruby couldn't help but laugh. "I'm really sorry; please don't feel obliged to do anything she asks. She's got her own ideas about how things work."

"I don't feel obliged at all. In fact it's about time someone was honest about the horrible condition of our cakes," he laughed and for the first time since Jacob's letter Ruby felt like maybe there was something to look forward to after all.

Elizabeth returned with the cakes one by one. Before long they were all on the counter with Daniel testing each one in turn. When he came to the last one, the coffee surprise, his eyes widened before they closed. He sighed contently and opened them, focusing on Ruby. "You're hired. When do you start?"

"*Nee, nee*. You misunderstood," Elizabeth said before Ruby could speak. "She's not coming to work for you. You're simply going to buy her cakes."

"That can work for me as well. What are you charging?"

Ruby, flummoxed for a moment, quickly calculated the average cost of baking a cake. She added a percentage profit and named her price.

Daniel laughed, "That's ridiculous."

Her smile fell until Daniel named an amount almost double her own. "I sell them per slice so you make more profit. And your cakes are worth that."

Surprised, elated and shocked, Ruby smiled. "*Denke*."

"Can I order one of each now?" Daniel said, opening his cash register. "I prefer paying upfront, that way I know I'll get my order on time."

As he handed her the bills, Ruby had to stop her jaw from dropping. "*Jah*, of course."

"Your cakes," Daniel said when she turned to leave.

Ruby smiled broadly with the wad of cash in her hands. "Keep them."

"See," Elizabeth said as they headed out of the store. "I told you I always have *gut* plans. Now you're not only gainfully employed, you're gainfully self-employed."

Ruby stopped in the middle of the sidewalk and drew Elizabeth into a hug. "*Denke*, for everything."

"It's a pleasure," Elizabeth said with a smile. "You can buy me a candy bar if you can spare the change."

Ruby laughed. "I'll buy you a box."

## Chapter Eleven

"**I**'m so glad you came today," Mary said, reaching into the basket for a biscuit. "I've been so worried about you. You haven't even been to Sunday Singings since Ruby left."

It was the first time since the break up that Mary managed to get Jacob to spend time with her. Up until now all her attempts had been fruitless. Every time he either had an excuse or simply told her he wasn't feeling up to it.

But when he agreed to join her on the picnic today, she knew that there was still hope for them. She knew that it would take time for Jacob to realize that they were meant to be together, but for that to happen they needed to spend time together.

"Have you had any news from Ohio?" Jacob asked glancing into the distance.

Mary had known the question would come and she had already prepared an answer. "Only that Ruby is happy and attending singings."

Jacob's brow rose, "Attending singings?"

"*Jah, Mamm* says she got over the broken engagement

very soon." Mary held the container of biscuits for Jacob.

He glanced at the biscuits and shook his head. "I just can't believe…never mind. I should have expected it."

"Exactly," Mary said firmly. "Let's not waste another minute talking about my traitorous *schweschder*. Let's rather enjoy our afternoon like we used before you and she got engaged."

Jacob nodded and reached for a biscuit. "You're right. I should stop trying to find a reason for what she did. She did and it's done. It's time to move on with my life. Tell me, how is your quilting going?"

Mary beamed when his attention turned to her instead of the landscape. "Very well, *denke*. I have five farm stalls that now buy my quilts. I have orders that should keep me busy for another month at least."

"That's *wunderbaar*. You always were a very good seamstress. Your parents must be very proud."

Mary nodded, "They are. *Mamm* says my *family*e will be very blessed one day to have a talented seamstress to sew their clothes."

"She's right," Jacob nodded with a ghost of a smile.

"How is the carpentry business? Do you still enjoy it?"

Jacob nodded, "Very much so. After… I've made a lot of pieces in the last few weeks. Enough that *Daed* could send them to other stores as well."

"Jacob, that's fantastic." Mary waited a moment and wondered how she was going to phrase her next words. "I wonder sometimes if everything happens for a reason. If…you know…we wouldn't have had this picnic, you wouldn't have made so many pieces, Ruby wouldn't have been happy in Ohio… Maybe this is the way it was really meant to be."

She watched a sadness flash in Jacob's eyes before he met her gaze again. "You might be right, but that still doesn't explain why Ruby did it. I've gone over it a hundred times in my mind and I keep getting to the same conclusion. I can't picture Ruby doing something like that, not the Ruby I love."

Mary didn't miss the present tense of the word love. She jumped up quickly and began slapping at her ankle. "I think something bit me. Jacob, quick, look if you see something."

Jacob leaned forward and looked at her ankle. "I don't see anything. Does it sting?"

"*Jah*, pretty badly."

In her mind she pictured Jacob scooping her up and carrying her back to his buggy. Instead, he reached into the basket for a bottle of water. "Here, this should help soothe it until you get home."

Mary clenched her teeth. She knew she needed to be patient, but Ruby had been gone for almost a month. How much longer did she need to wait for Jacob to realize what was right before his eyes?

"*Denke*, Jacob," she purred. "You're so thoughtful."

Jacob smiled at the compliment before reaching for another biscuit. One way or another, Mary decided, she would make him come to Sunday singings again and when he did she would make certain that he offered her a ride home, even if she had to break a spoke on the buggy wheel herself.

## Chapter Twelve

Ruby's heart skipped a beat as she walked into Fischer's bakery a few weeks later. Ever since Elizabeth's forceful visit, she had baked for Daniel Fischer every week. Ruby couldn't help but wonder if it was simply because the poor man had been intimidated by her mother's cousin, or if he really liked her baking.

Today was the first time Elizabeth didn't accompany her to town, and today she wanted to make it clear to the attractive proprietor that he was under no obligation to buy her cakes. She stacked two cake tins one on top of the other and headed into the bakery. She would return for the others in a little while.

Daniel stood by the glass confectionary display case helping a customer when she walked in. He smiled at her and lifted a hand in greeting. Ruby couldn't help but return the smile. The few times she had seen Daniel, she couldn't help but notice how attractive he was. He was friendly to old and young alike who entered his store, and more surprising than anything, he didn't seem to mind Elizabeth's steamrolling manner.

With the amount of money Daniel was paying for

the cakes she baked, she had already saved up a significant amount to send home to her parents. She knew they didn't expect her to send them money, but she had relied on them for so many years, it only felt right to return the favor.

After setting the two tins on the counter, Ruby went back for the rest. It took three trips in total to bring all the cakes into the shop. She was about to wave Daniel goodbye, thinking she'd get her money next week rather than interrupt him, when he turned the customer over to one of the assistants.

"Hullo, Ruby. Sorry about that, it's been a busier day than usual, but you're just in time."

Ruby frowned, noticing the cakes left over in the confectionary display. "In time for what?"

"For me to take my lunch. Care to join me? I have a penchant for something that isn't sweet. How about we go to the diner and indulge in a hamburger and fries."

His invitation was so lighthearted, his smile so genuine, that Ruby found herself agreeing to her own surprise. "That sounds nice."

"Great, just give me a minute." She watched as Daniel instructed one of the assistants before removing his apron. Within minutes he had his wide brim hat on and had joined her on the other side of the counter. "How have you been?"

The personal question caught her off guard for a moment before she remembered he didn't know anything about Jacob or their breakup. "I've been very well, *denke*. Holmes County has charmed me, I must admit."

Daniel nodded as he opened the door for her. "It's been my home all my life and I can't imagine living anywhere else. You're from Lancaster, right?"

*"Jah."* Ruby found herself relaxing as they walked along the sidewalk to the diner a few blocks away. Daniel kept asking questions but she found herself wanting to answer, just like she wanted to know more about him.

After finding a seat in a booth, they placed an order for a cheeseburger and fries each before Daniel turned to her again. "Your aunt is quite chatty. She came in the other day and told me a little more about you."

Ruby felt her cheeks turn ruby red at the thought of Elizabeth discussing her with others. "She did?"

*"Jah,"* and you don't have to look so frightened. She didn't tell me about your warts and bad habits." Daniel laughed easily. "She just told me you came to Ohio to heal from heartbreak."

Ruby's brows shot up. "I'm sorry, she shouldn't have." Ruby began to stand up when Daniel's warm hand closed over hers.

"I didn't say that to embarrass you. I merely said it because I can't understand what type of *mann* lets a girl like you slip through his fingers. Besides your baking, you've charmed me already."

Ruby smiled, realizing she didn't want to leave after all. "It's a long story, but you're right. I needed to get away."

"Well, that's lucky for Fischer's Amish Bakery, because I've never sold so much cake in my life."

"About that. Elizabeth meant well, truly she has a good soul, but don't feel you have to sell my cakes simply because she bulldozed you into it. I'm sure your cakes weren't as dry, crumbly or tasteless as she said."

Daniel sighed heavily, shaking his head before he

leaned closer over the table. "To be honest. It was worse, she was being kind."

Ruby expected him to admit he didn't want to sell her cakes, she didn't expect humor and mischief to twinkle in his gaze. "You're not like any other *mann* I've met before, Daniel." The words were out of her mouth before she even realized she thought them.

Daniel laughed, "*Denke*, I'll take that as a compliment. You're like no other girl as well. Maybe, if you have the time and your boss isn't too demanding, we could have lunch again next week."

Ruby found herself agreeing once again. "I'd like that. But only if you tell me how a young *mann* came to own a bakery."

"It's simply, actually. My *daed* was a baker, of bread mostly, *Mamm* baked cakes and pastries. When our kitchen became too small, they opened the shop in town. A few years ago *Daed* passed after suffering a heart attack, and *Mamm* passed last year after a short struggle with cancer. Now I run and own a bakery."

The words were easy but Ruby could see the memory of the loss wasn't. This time she found herself reaching for his hand and squeezing it. "I'm sorry for your loss, Daniel. I'm sure they would have been very proud of what you've achieved."

"I'm sure they would, especially since I found you."

The moment deepened with the promise of more than friendship. Ruby never thought she would seek out love or a relationship but looking into Daniel's sky-blue eyes made her realize she could still dream.

Right now she was dreaming of a future with a man like Daniel.

For a brief moment she remembered Jacob and his

letter. The memory used to bring a sting of pain that shot through her heart, now it was only a faint twinge.

She smiled as the waiter arrived with their order. She knew in her heart there was still the lingering love for Jacob and what they had shared, but she also knew in her mind that Jacob had turned his back on her.

Was it possible for her to find love here in Holmes County, or was she simply reading more into Daniel's friendly disposition?

## Chapter Thirteen

Her first month in Ohio was an adjustment. Ruby missed home, she missed her family and most of all she missed Jacob.

Baking for Fischer's Amish Bakery had helped her in more ways than she could imagine. Not only could she bake to her heart's content without worrying about the cost of ingredients, she had the company of Elizabeth to constantly cheer her up.

Spring had turned to summer, which was slowly receding, allowing autumn to take its grasp on Ohio. The leaves had turned, the lush green fields turned to gold and brown but her heart was blooming like a fresh flower in spring.

A smile lifted the corners of Ruby's mouth as she drove the buggy into town. After Daniel's first lunch invitation, it had become a weekly event. Every week when she delivered the cakes, Daniel took her to lunch.

At first she had kept her lunches with Daniel a secret from Elizabeth until one day when Elizabeth had gone into town with Ruby. She could still remember Elizabeth's laughter when Daniel had sounded very disappointed that they wouldn't be going to lunch.

Elizabeth had pretended to have a few errands to run in town and promised to meet Ruby back at the bakery in an hour. Ruby had expected teasing, she had expected Elizabeth to write her mother about the blooming romance between her and the baker, but Elizabeth had done nothing of the sort. Instead she had encouraged Ruby to find her heart and her happiness in the same place. Words Ruby remembered every day since.

After a few lunches, Daniel had invited Ruby to Sunday singings at their church, and of course he had asked her to ride home with him every time. It was new, it was exciting; but more than that, it felt right.

Ruby knew she was falling in love with Daniel even though she wasn't sure she had fallen out of love with Jacob just yet. This thought remained on her mind as she walked into the bakery today. She found it oddly quiet and the door was closed. Peering inside, she noticed that Daniel was alone there. He rushed to the door and relieved her of the cake tins. "Like always, just on time." Daniel smiled in greeting.

"Where is everyone?" Ruby asked, confused at the silence.

"I gave them the afternoon off. I need to do some accounting later this afternoon, but first I planned on us having lunch here today."

Ruby couldn't stop the smile that spread across her face as she noticed the neatly laid table in the corner.

"I made us pies and of course there is cake for dessert," Daniel said before putting down the cake tins.

"Daniel, you've gone to so much trouble," Ruby said, shaking her head. She knew their relationship was growing by the minute and every time she thought she couldn't fall deeper in love with Daniel, he did something that made her heart leap with love.

"You deserve every ounce of trouble and more." Daniel held out a chair for her. "*Kumm*, sit."

Ruby took a seat and a grin formed on her mouth as she noticed the fresh flowers on the table. "This is really special."

"I was hoping it would be," Daniel said with a nervous look. "Look, I've never done this before so please correct me if I'm doing this wrong. Since the first time you walked into the bakery, I knew you were meant for me. I know it sounds foolish, but not as foolish as I felt the first time you smiled at me. Over the last few months, I've realized that I've never thought of having a *familye* or planning a future because I've never found the right girl. I know your home is in Lancaster and I know some time you plan on returning." Daniel took a deep breath and Ruby frowned as her insides began to twist nervously.

"Daniel, what are you saying?" Ruby asked carefully.

"I'm saying, don't go back. I'm saying stay and start a *familye* with me, plan a future with me, bake cakes with me. I love you, Ruby King, and I plan on spending the rest of my life proving to you just how much."

The question caught her off guard, the declaration made her gasp. Ruby shook her head slowly. "It's only been a few months…"

Jacob had courted her for years and suddenly all of this was happening too fast.

"I found my happiness when I lost my heart on you. I only needed a minute to know that." Daniel reached for her hand. "I know it's fast, I know it's sudden, but I also know this is right."

Ruby cleared her throat, unable to form any words. She took a deep cleansing breath. Suddenly everything about Jacob came rushing back. Their courtship, their friendship, the breakup that tore her heart to pieces. Was she really ready to go through all that again?

"I know that you were hurt in Lancaster, but I can promise you I won't hurt you. I love you..." Daniel's voice softened, his eyes grew a deeper shade of blue as they pleaded for an answer.

Ruby slowly shook her head. "I'm not saying *nee*, Daniel, but I am saying I need to think about this first. I didn't expect...you caught me completely off guard. I haven't even thought of the future yet."

Daniel nodded with a small smile playing on his lips. "I'm asking you to think about it now. I can see I've shocked you, so let's put that aside and enjoy our lunch."

Ruby did just that but when she arrived home it only took one look for Elizabeth to know something was wrong. "What happened?"

Ruby considered lying, but Elizabeth had become much more than just her mother's cousin. Elizabeth had become her best friend since she arrived in Holmes County. "Daniel asked me to marry him."

"What?" Elizabeth clapped her hands together with glee. "That's *wunderbaar*. Ach, he is such a *gut mann*, Ruby, you are truly blessed to have his affections."

Ruby nodded slowly, she still couldn't fathom what had just happened.

"What's the problem?"

"What do you mean?" Ruby asked confused.

"I can see from your expression you didn't say *jah*, so why didn't you?"

Ruby sighed, "I just kept thinking about Jacob. We courted for years. We had our whole future planned until he broke up with me. On the one hand, I'm sure I do not want my heart broken again and on the other, I'm not sure I'm not still in love with Jacob."

Elizabeth nodded slowly, "Firstly, Daniel wouldn't break your heart. I've got a good handle on these things and he won't say anything he doesn't mean. Secondly, I don't think you're still in love with Jacob, I just think the memory of the love you had for him will always be there. If you still loved Jacob, how could you have fallen in love with Daniel?"

Elizabeth's words rang true. Perhaps it was the memory of her love for Jacob that held her back instead of actual love. She closed her eyes and tried to see into her future. For the first time in years it wasn't Jacob swinging their toddler in the air.

It was Daniel.

## Chapter Fourteen

Mary knew it was going to be a difficult conversation but she also knew it wasn't one she could delay forever if she wanted to be married before the New Year. Ever since their first picnic together, she and Jacob had spent more and more time together.

Over the course of a month, they had started attending singings together and riding home without anyone knowing they were courting. Everything was falling into place for her, absolutely everything.

Not only had Ruby not yet returned from Ohio, but Jacob mentioned her name less and less these days.

Last night after singing she had approached the subject first. "Jacob, do you ever think of the future?"

Jacob had been startled by her question at first until he stopped the buggy and turned to her. "The future?"

"*Jah*, you know. Us? We've been courting for almost three months now."

Jacob nodded but he didn't smile. "I...you're right, we have been courting," he said as if it was news to him.

Mary smiled sweetly and shifted a little closer. "Wedding season is coming up soon, Jacob, and I think there will be no better ending to this year than us ending it together."

Jacob's eyes narrowed for a moment before he grinned. "You're right, we should announce our engagement."

Mary didn't know if he agreed simply because she cornered him or because he truly wanted to marry her. But she did know that he still thought about Ruby. There were moments like last night after they spoke of an engagement that he would grow quiet and Mary would know he was thinking about her sister.

The sooner they announced their engagement the sooner they could get married, Mary reasoned. Once they were married he would forget all about Ruby and their long ago engagement. He would have a wife and a family to focus on, and Mary wanting nothing more.

She walked into the kitchen knowing both her parents would be surprised at her news, but she knew the sooner she told them the better. She smiled broadly as she sat down at the dinner table. Her mother was the first to take the bait.

"Mary, what on earth are you so happy about?" Anna King asked with a curious smile.

"*Mamm, Daed*, I have some news," Mary started before she took a deep breath. "I'm engaged!"

Her mother's eyes widened as she jumped up and moved towards her daughter. After wrapping her in a warm hug, she stood back allowing her husband to hug their daughter as well.

"Congratulations, my dear *dochder*. I knew the day would come when you met the right *mann*. Do we know him?" her mother asked eagerly.

"This is truly the best news after the year we've had. Who is it?" David King interrupted.

Mary smiled, swallowing past the nervous bundle in her throat. "It's Jacob. Jacob Schrock."

"What!" her father shouted. "How can you even think of marrying Jacob? When did you even start courting?"

"David, give her a chance to explain," Anna urged her husband although Mary could see her mother was just as surprised.

"About a month after Ruby left. He was devastated, *Daed*. We've been friends for so long, I wanted to support him. One thing led to another and before we knew it, we had fallen in love."

Anna sighed heavily as she shook her head. "I cannot understand how you can allow the boy to court you who broke your *schweschder's* heart. We had to send her to Ohio to find herself again and now you tell us you want us to forgive him and accept him."

"*Mamm*, what happened between him and Ruby has nothing to do with me. Should I turn away my happiness simply because you chose to promise the wrong *dochder*? This isn't my fault; it's your fault for arranging a marriage between them. If you had chosen me instead, none of this would have happened."

Anna gasped audibly at her daughter's outburst but Mary ignored it. She was done bending to her parents' will and Ruby's happiness. Why couldn't they be happy for her? Why couldn't they congratulate her and invite him over for dinner like they did when Ruby had been courted by Jacob?

It seemed there were double standards and Mary was tired of it. She loved Jacob Schrock with all her heart and right now she didn't care whether or not her parents approved.

"It's just a shock to us, that's all," her mother tried to placate her, but Mary didn't miss the hard look her father gave her.

"*Daed*, are you mad at me?" Mary asked forcing a smile.

"*Nee*, I'm not mad. I'm disappointed. I didn't think Jacob would try and weasel his way into this *familye* again after what happened."

Mary shrugged, "We're in love and I'd appreciate it if you could respect that."

With that, Mary turned and left the room. It was time her parents realized that she deserved to be happy as well. She worked long and hard for this to finally happen. She had watched her sister's heart break; she had sat by while Jacob grieved over the wrong girl. This was her time and she wasn't going to let anyone, or anything get in her way.

## Chapter Fifteen

David watched his eldest daughter rush out of the kitchen. Something about this entire conversation didn't sit right with him. The part about them making a mistake and promising the wrong daughter made him think.

It brought ugly thoughts into his mind about what his daughter could have been capable of. Ever since he had confronted Jacob, he had wondered about the source Jacob had mentioned. In his heart he knew Ruby would have never cheated on Jacob with an *Englischer*, but up until now he had no idea who would have put that thought into Jacob's mind.

He thought about Ruby who was still in Ohio. She had left home a broken girl, devastated by Jacob's action. He was grateful to Elizabeth for taking Ruby under her wing and, over the last few months, it seemed his daughter was back to her cheerful self again, but that didn't erase the past.

"I can't believe it," Anna said, shaking her head. "Jacob Schrock. Of all the *menner* in Lancaster, she had to fall in love with the one that drove Ruby from her home."

David sighed, knowing his wife was right. None of this seemed right and he was about to find out the truth. "If you'll excuse me I have some things in the barn I need to see to."

He crossed his fingers, hoping his wife wouldn't question him as he walked out the kitchen door. He knew that Mary always climbed on top of the lumber pile behind the barn when she was upset. He found her there staring at the stars.

"*Daed*? If you've come to apologize, I'm still too angry." Her words were as biting as her tone of voice. For the first time David allowed himself to admit that his eldest daughter was a disappointment to him. For years he had ignored her biting words, her selfish ways and her condescending treatment of others, but now it was easy to admit as she glared down at him from the top of the lumber pile.

"I didn't come to apologize," David said through clenched teeth. "I came to find out the truth. I know why Jacob broke up with Ruby. He told me months ago."

Just as he had assumed, her brows rose with surprise, but she quickly masked it with a disappointed look. "I know, he told me as well. It was truly horrible of Ruby to cheat on him with an *Englischer.*"

"Only," David said, climbing onto the lumber pile. "I don't believe she did. Jacob mentioned a reliable source when he told me the story. He said someone he trusted with his life told him of this. Someone he'd known for years."

"I have no idea who told him," Mary quickly retreated but the fear shone in her eyes.

David took a seat beside her and turned to her with a heavy sigh. "I asked around about the *Englischer* and no one knew what I was talking about. You know what I think, Mary? I think that you were jealous of your *schweschder*. You were jealous of her relationship with Jacob and you told him a lie to make sure he didn't go through with the wedding. Sending your *schweschder* to Ohio fell in perfectly with your plan because you had Jacob all to yourself."

"*Daed*," the determination in her eyes turned to sadness. "You have to understand. I didn't want to hurt her, they weren't right for each other."

"What I understand is that my one *dochder* couldn't stand seeing her *schweschder* happy. In the process she told lies and almost ruined her *schweschder's* life to get her own way. I'm very disappointed, that's all I will say of this. I've had enough of lies and betrayal for a lifetime, after what you did."

David stood up and heard Mary begin to cry. The father inside him wanted to turn around and wrap his daughter in his arms, to take away her sadness. But the other part of him knew what she had done was unforgivable. It was ruthless and conniving and he was disappointed to know she had been capable of it.

"I only did it because I loved Jacob. I always have. But you promised him to Ruby. After that day he only had eyes for her. I knew it was wrong, I knew I would hurt Ruby, but I couldn't stop it. I love Jacob; I couldn't stand the thought of losing him to Ruby."

"Did you for one minute consider that he loved Ruby? That not only did you break your *schweschder's* heart, but you broke his as well. How do you even know he loves you? Aren't you just the consolation prize now that Ruby is gone?"

Mary's eyes widened and she sniffed suddenly. "*Nee*, don't say that. Jacob loves me."

"We'll know when I tell him the truth." David turned and walked away. He never thought the day would come that he would look at his eldest daughter with disgust and disappointment, but right now he couldn't even look at her at all.

He walked back into the kitchen and sat down with a heavy sigh before turning to his wife. It was time Anna knew the events that had led to their one daughter's heartbreak and another's engagement.

## Chapter Sixteen

For almost a week, the tension in the King home was palpable until David realized what Mary had done would hang like a dark cloud over them until things were set right. He wasn't about to write to his daughter to tell her of her sister's betrayal, but he knew it was time Jacob Schrock knew the truth.

He discussed it with Anna who agreed that Ruby's name should be cleared with Jacob. Mary kept to herself, barely talking or meeting his gaze. David could see his daughter was repenting for her sins but he found it harder than ever before to forgive.

How could he forgive such a thing?

He prayed for guidance every night, hoping that God would help him ease the hardness he felt towards his daughter. He sat for hours thinking about Mary when she was a little girl and the more he thought about it the more he realized Mary had always been jealous of Ruby.

Surely sibling rivalry was normal, David reasoned, he just never realized how far Ruby would be willing to take it.

David flicked the reins, needing the horse to go

faster. The longer it took him to get to Jacob, the more time there was to change his mind. It was the first time in his life than he needed to hang his head for something his daughter had done and he wasn't looking forward to the moment.

He could see in his wife's eyes how much Mary's betrayal hurt her, how disappointed she was in her eldest daughter, but David knew Anna found forgiveness easier in her heart than he did.

The horse turned into the small dirt road leading to Jacob's home and David took a deep breath. It was late afternoon and he hoped Jacob's father would have already headed inside, leaving Jacob alone in the work shed. This conversation did not need anyone as witness to his daughter's conniving nature.

David climbed out of the buggy and heard the saw chewing its way through a piece of lumber. He sent up a quick prayer for guidance and strength and pushed open the door.

"Mr. King?" Jacob asked, surprised by David's entrance.

David forced a smile, "That's a nice piece of lumber you got there. What are your plans with it?"

"Dining room table," Jacob frowned. "I'm sure you're not here to discuss my furniture designs. Is something wrong?"

David laughed wryly. Was it that obvious? "I need to talk to you about something. Not that I want to, but I think it's imperative that you know the truth."

"The truth about what?" Jacob set down the saw and wiped his hands on a cloth before he walked towards David.

"Mind if I take a seat?" David sat down on the make-shift bench against the wall.

"I'm listening," Jacob said, taking a seat across from him.

"You remember you told me you had it from a re-liable source that Ruby was cheating on you with an *Englischer*."

David watched the younger man's jaw clench. "It's not something I'm fond of remembering. It's been al-most six months; it's time for me to move on."

David nodded, "Before you move on, you need to know this. I know your 'source' was Mary."

Jacob sighed, "It must have pained her to bring that information to me. But she kept me from making a mistake."

For a brief moment David searched Jacob's eyes. When he had spoken of Ruby, his eyes had softened but nothing changed at the mention of Mary. His heart clenched realizing that perhaps Mary had lied about the engagement as well. "She lied." The words tasted bitter on his tongue as a sigh escaped.

"What do you mean?" Jacob shook his head. "I know Ruby lied. She never once admitted to it. In fact, I made sure she didn't have a chance to plead her case with me. That's why I wrote the letter."

David met Jacob's confused gaze, "Ruby didn't lie, Jacob. Mary did."

Jacob felt his heart skip a beat. The events of a few months ago all came rushing back with the force of a hurricane. Mary's confession about her sister's infidel-ity. His insistence not to see Ruby again. The broken engagement. Ruby's departure to Ohio.

None of it made sense. "Why do you say Mary lied?"

For the first time he noticed the shadows around David's eyes, the tired look in his gaze. "Because she admitted it to me. She's been jealous of Ruby her entire life. I had a suspicion, but I never thought she would do something to harm her *schweschder*. Their mother and I merely put it down to sibling rivalry. Apparently we underestimated Mary."

Jacob stood up, needing to move to process the blow that had just been given. "Mary lied about Ruby and the *Englischer*?"

"There never was an *Englischer*."

"You mean…" Jacob frowned as anger quickly seeped into his bloodstream, reaching almost boiling point. "You mean that Mary came to me with a story about an *Englischer* because she hoped I would break up with Ruby? Because she was jealous of Ruby and me?"

David nodded. "Apparently she wanted to be the one betrothed to you. I know right now you're angry as a spitting cobra, but I need you to understand she did it because she believed she was doing the right thing."

"How is that possible?" Jacob shouted, slamming his fist against the wall. "She ruined our relationship. She made me doubt every minute I spent falling in love with Ruby. She made me hate Ruby. For heaven's sake, Mr. King, you sent Ruby away because of it. How could she have thought she was doing the right thing?"

Jacob's vision blurred; his eyes red-rimmed. He couldn't believe that Mary had taken it upon herself to ruin his life. The future he had planned with Ruby was flushed down the drain because of Mary's words. He had trusted her. She was Ruby's sister; he had no reason not to.

"I know. In her own twisted way she thought she

was righting a wrong. She says she's loved you forever and couldn't stand the thought of seeing you marrying Ruby. Her jealousy is sinful, I know that, but I also need you to understand she did it because she loved you."

Jacob's jaw dropped. "Mary loves me?"

"*Jah*, she told us about your engagement a few days ago."

Jacob laughed, the cynical sound filling the small work shed. "Engagement? I'm sorry to say but that's simply another one of her lies. I've always been fond of Mary, we've been friends since I can remember, but love… I'm sorry, Mr. King, but I've never loved Mary. I don't know where she got that impression. We're simply friends, always have been, always will be. I've never loved Mary the way I loved Ruby."

David pinched the bridge of his nose. "I thought as much but I needed to hear it from you first. I'm really sorry about this, David. This whole misunderstanding…"

"It wasn't a misunderstanding; it was lies and deceit. Does Ruby know?"

"*Nee*. I didn't think it was the type of thing to tell her in a letter. She would be shattered by her *schweschder's* betrayal. She seems to have moved on from all this. She's happy in Ohio; I don't want to bring her sadness again."

"She needs to know and I'm going to tell her. Could you tell me where she is in Ohio?" Jacob already had a plan in mind. If he finished here and packed tonight, he could take the first bus to Ohio in the morning. If all went well, he could have Ruby back in his arms by tomorrow evening.

David shook his head, "Jacob, is this really a *gut* idea. So much time has passed…"

"*Jah*, it is a *gut* idea. Time might have passed, but not even that has changed my feelings for Ruby. We were meant to be together. We had our future mapped out when Mary came to me with that story. I won't let her lies and jealousy stand in the way of our happiness. I need to talk to Ruby and you're right, this isn't something you say in a letter."

He waited a few moments while David debated before he finally looked up. "Do you have a pen and paper?"

Jacob walked towards the table where they kept their orders. A few minutes later he had Ruby's address in his hands and hope in his heart. "I know how hard this must have been for you, Mr. King, but I want to thank you for having the courage to tell me."

David nodded with a heavy sigh. "When will you be leaving?"

"Tomorrow. Can I ask you one last favor before you go?"

"*Jah*, of course."

"Tell Mary if she ever comes near me again I'll put in a request with the bishop to put her on notice." He knew it was a brash favor, one that could get Mary shunned but he didn't want any further part in her lies and deceit.

"I'll make sure this stops here," David confirmed before standing up and returning his wide brim hat to his head. "Tell Ruby we send our love."

Jacob nodded and watched David walk out of the shed. He turned and looked at the piece he was busy with. It could wait.

Everything could wait until he had Ruby back in his life.

# Chapter Seventeen

Ruby had just finished cleaning the kitchen after a lovely dinner of beef stew when there was a knock on the door. The sun had already begun its descent into the west, the night creeping closer. A frown creased her brow when the knock sounded again.

"Are you expecting company?" Elizabeth asked from the door.

Ruby shook her head, "*Nee*. Daniel would never visit unless invited."

"Well then, we'd better see who it is. Maybe there's an emergency at the neighbors."

Ruby nodded as she moved towards the door. She unlocked and carefully opened it. Peering through the narrow opening, she didn't recognize him at first.

"Ruby?"

Her heart skipped a beat as her head moved from side to side. "Jacob?"

"*Jah*, it's me. I'm sorry to bother you so late."

"Ruby, who is it?" Elizabeth called from the kitchen even as Ruby tried to fathom why Jacob Schrock would turn up on her doorstep in Ohio.

"It's…uh…it's Jacob Schrock, from Lancaster," Ruby said as she opened the door a little wider.

Within seconds Elizabeth was by her side. "Would you like me to send him away?" she asked firmly. Over time Ruby had shared with Elizabeth the story about her and Jacob.

"Please, ma'am. Don't send me away. I just want a few minutes to talk to Ruby, and then I'll be on my way. Please Ruby, just a few minutes."

Ruby couldn't help but be intrigued. For almost a month Jacob had refused to talk to her. For more than six months she hadn't heard a single word from him. Now he had come all the way to Ohio. Either he had a good reason, or something was wrong back home. "It's alright, Elizabeth, I'll talk to him."

Elizabeth gave Jacob a hard look before turning to Ruby. "I'll be in my room if you need me."

Ruby nodded and stood aside for Jacob to enter. He looked just as handsome as she remembered but seeing him brought back the pain and the memories of the letter that had broken her heart. Feeling nervous, she led him into the kitchen. "*Kaffe?*"

"*Jah*, please. I didn't realize it was such a long trip."

Ruby didn't answer. She wasn't the one who had just crossed state lines to have a conversation. In fact, after all these months she still couldn't believe Jacob had broken her heart without a single explanation. She made the coffee and joined him at the table, waiting to hear what he had to say.

She listened as Jacob explained about the rumor of the *Englischer*, his disappointment and the letter that followed. A frown creased her brow, knowing that she had never cheated on Jacob. She couldn't help but feel fresh anger rush up, knowing that he had believed a rumor instead of asking her directly.

"I think you should leave now," she said quietly, not wanting to hear any more about his distrust in her.

"*Nee*, not yet. I haven't finished. Your father came to see me yesterday, Ruby. It was all lies, and I was fool enough to believe them. I lost you because I believed a liar over you. I made a mistake, Ruby, I intend to fix it."

"Who did you believe? Why did my father come to see you?" Ruby asked, even more confused. Who would spread such evil lies about her?

"Mary," Jacob finished quietly. "Your father says she told them that I asked her to marry me, another lie. Apparently she had been jealous of you for years and she couldn't stand the thought of us getting married."

Shock, disappointment and anger fought for precedence as Ruby tried to understand. "So you're telling me that my own *schweschder* lied about me cheating on you, and you believed her."

"I was a *dummkopf*, Ruby. You have to know how much I mean that. I threw away everything we had because of a lie. I'm asking you to come home, Ruby. Don't let Mary's lies influence our future for another moment. Please, let's put it behind us and announce. We can announce on Sunday."

Ruby shook her head very slowly. She had built a new life for herself here in Ohio. She had fallen in love with a wonderful man. For months she had wondered if she really loved Daniel. With Jacob she had been certain of her love. It was too much, she couldn't think with Jacob sitting across from her.

"I need to think about this, Jacob. It's all very sudden. I can't...you need to go now."

The words were barely out of her mouth before Elizabeth stood in the doorway. "There's a nice little lodge in town where you can stay. I believe Ruby asked you to leave."

Jacob glanced at Ruby one last time before he stood up and let himself out. As soon as the door clicked shut, the tears began to stream over her face.

She had wondered for months why Jacob had broken up with her, only to find out it was her own sister's doing. As she cried she felt Elizabeth's arm wrap around her shoulders. "It's alright, Ruby, everything will be alright."

At Elizabeth's consoling words, she cried even harder. How could everything be alright? She had moved away to heal her heart, only to meet Daniel. How could she even think of reconciling with Jacob after falling in love with Daniel?

She knew the real question she had to ask herself, but she was afraid of the answer.

Who did she truly love?

## Chapter Eighteen

Ruby ordered water.

The waitress walked away, and she glanced at the diner's entrance, waiting for Jacob to arrive. She had taken a day to think about what he said and knew the sooner she spoke with him, the better. Daniel didn't know about Jacob's arrival in Ohio.

The diner's doors opened and Jacob walked in. A smile spread across his face as he made his way towards Ruby.

"I'm so happy you asked to meet me. I knew you would understand."

Ruby forced a smile on her face. Ever since his visit to Elizabeth's house two nights before, Ruby had taken the time to search her heart. For months she had been convinced that she could never love Daniel as she loved Jacob. In the early hours of this morning the realization had dawned on her.

She didn't love Daniel like Jacob, she loved him more. Her love for Daniel was like a tree, it was steadfast and strong. Her love for Jacob had been the love of a young bloom. It withered without her even realizing it.

"I do understand, Jacob," Ruby began as the waitress returned with her water. "I understand now that even after everything we shared and planned, you took my *schweschder*'s word over mine. Instead of coming to me to ask for the truth, you wrote me a letter without any explanation. You didn't trust me enough to ask me the truth."

"I should have… I know that now," Jacob pleaded.

"*Jah*, you should have. But you see, you didn't. I was broken, Jacob. All our dreams shattered in the wind without even a simple explanation, because you didn't trust me. I came to Ohio to heal and I did; but I also met a *mann* who loves me. A *mann* who trusts me and wants to marry me. Up until today, I didn't think I loved him enough, but I realize now that I do."

"What? There's someone else?" The surprise in his expression was clear but Ruby ignored it. She wouldn't feel guilty for falling in love after what Jacob had done.

"There is. And seeing you again, hearing the truth about what happened, only made me realize how much I love him. I appreciate you coming here to explain. I forgive you for not trusting me, but I cannot pick up and go back to Lancaster as if nothing happened. Everything happened. I learned I can't trust a *mann* who doesn't trust me. I can't love a *mann* who listens to others over me. I've changed and my heart now belongs to another. I'm not going back to Lancaster, Jacob."

"Are you staying here? But your home, your *familye*, is in Lancaster?" Jacob argued.

Ruby shook her head, "My *familye* and my childhood home will always be in Lancaster, but my heart and my future is in Ohio. I know you must be in a hurry to get back home so I won't keep you any longer. The bus leaves in an hour if you want to go home today. Can I ask you to make sure my *schweschder* gets this letter?"

Jacob shook his head, "I'm not giving up on you, Ruby. We had a future, we have our past, we can't just let Mary come between us."

Ruby sighed as she pulled the letter out of her bag, "Mary didn't come between us, Jacob. The fact that you didn't trust me did. Life is bound to be filled with more challenges and I don't want to face those challenges with someone who didn't come to me at the first sign of trouble. That's all I will say about this. I'm putting it behind me and you should as well. Let's learn from this instead of letting it haunt our future. Will you make sure Mary gets the letter?"

Jacob stood up, shaking his head, "I just came all this way to tell you the truth, and now you're sending me away with a letter for your traitorous *schweschder*?"

"I'm sending you away with gratitude and asking for a favor," Ruby could see he was angered by her refusal to take him back, but she didn't let that change her mind. She knew where her heart was and where it would remain.

Jacob snapped the letter up and walked out of the diner without saying goodbye.

Ruby finished drinking her water, leaving a tip for the waitress while she thought over the letter for Mary. She had written it early this morning and hoped that Mary would read it with the same open heart as it was written.

*Dear Mary,*

*I know what you did and I forgive you. I am happy in Ohio and in love with a wunderbaar mann. I*

*wish you the same happiness and love. Please
don't let your love for Jacob blind you to love
another. Find your happiness and when you do,
you'll realize your love for Jacob was never really real.*

*Much love
Ruby*

Ruby didn't feel the need to go into every little de-
tail. She didn't need to scold her sister for what she had
done. It wasn't her place to judge, only to accept and to
love. Forgiving Mary was going to be hard, but she'd remind herself of that letter every day until she no longer
felt anger and betrayal when she thought of her sister.

She walked to the bakery and a smile spread across
her face as she stepped inside. Daniel was helping a
little boy who was buying pastries. She walked up to
him and overheard how the little boy didn't have enough
money for the cake he wanted. Ruby walked around the
counter, opened the cake display and took out the plate.

Daniel frowned but didn't say a word as she walked
back around the counter to the little boy. "Here you go.
This one is on me. Don't drop it on your way home."

The little boy's face brightened up with surprise.
"For free?"

Ruby nodded with a gentle smile, "Today's your
lucky day."

A bubbly laughter escaped him as he rushed out of
the store to his mother who was waiting in a buggy
outside. Ruby turned to Daniel and felt the love over-
whelm her. How could she have doubted how much
she loved him? He was everything. He was her begin-

ning and her end, he was her future and her dreams all wrapped into one.

"You just made that little boy's day," Daniel laughed as he joined her on the other side of the counter.

"I'm about to make yours as well." Ruby smiled broadly as she took Daniel's hand. *"Jah."*

Daniel frowned before realization dawned in his gaze. "Really?"

*"Jah.* We'll need to get permission from our bishops; I'll need to talk to my *familye*, but *jah.* I will spend the rest of my life with you, Daniel Fischer."

Daniel wrapped his arms around her and swung her in a circle. "You didn't just make my day, you made my life." He laughed as he kept twirling her in the middle of the bakery.

## Chapter Nineteen

As autumn gave way to winter, Ruby and Daniel said their vows in Elizabeth's barn. Ruby's family travelled all the way from Lancaster to witness their daughter's wedding, even Mary. As a token of apology, she had sewed Ruby's wedding gown, just like they had planned when they were children.

Ruby baked a beautiful five layer cake, Daniel's favorite double chocolate of course, and the women in the community prepared the lunch.

As she said her vows to Daniel she knew that everything had happened for a reason. If she hadn't loved Jacob, she wouldn't have known her love for Daniel was stronger and more powerful. If Mary hadn't betrayed her she would have never come to Ohio. If she hadn't come to Ohio, she would have never met Elizabeth or Daniel.

Although the road to her happily ever after was tumultuous, often rocky, and sometimes bleak with sadness, the result was amazing.

After the wedding, Ruby had moved in with Daniel

but still visited Elizabeth on most days, often baking at her house simply to enjoy the pleasure of her company.

More than a year had passed since the day she had said her vows, and she still couldn't believe how happy she was. Not only was she swollen with her first child, but happiness seemed to find its way to her family as well.

Mary had finally met a nice young man from another community, Caleb Zook, and was engaged. Her parents were both elated at the thought of their first grandchild and were debating moving to Ohio as well. As for Jacob, things didn't turn out as well. After returning to Lancaster, he couldn't seem to get over Ruby and Mary's deceit. He moved to a small community just outside of New York and opened a furniture shop there.

Ruby often thought of him and prayed for him to find a good wife, but not once did she regret her decision.

As for Daniel, he couldn't be a more perfect husband if he tried. He treated Ruby like a princess and boasted about her baking skills to anyone who would listen. Ruby still wasn't the best housekeeper or seamstress but luckily she made enough by selling her cakes to pay a cleaning lady twice a week.

She didn't see it as laziness, rather as job creation. The cleaning lady was a young girl from the Amish community who cleaned for *Englischers* mostly, but two days a week she cleaned for the Fischers.

Over the last few days, Ruby knew Daniel had something up his sleeve. For some reason he asked her not to come into the store. He used her advanced pregnancy as an excuse but Ruby knew better. Her husband was up to something and she didn't have the foggiest idea what it could be.

She had asked Elizabeth if she knew, but even her friend was sworn to secrecy. When Daniel arrived home shortly after lunch, she couldn't help but be surprised. Daniel never came home for lunch, especially not on Fridays, their busiest day of the week.

"Come on, it's time you got out of the *haus* for a change," he said with a broad smile as he stepped into the kitchen.

Ruby cocked her hands on her hips. "I thought I was supposed to stay at home and wait for the *boppli*."

"You can wait for the *boppli* again tomorrow. *Kumm* on, hurry," David said almost bouncing with excitement. Ruby couldn't help but laugh at the sight of her husband.

"I'm coming, I'm coming," Ruby laughed, grabbing her purse and her coat as she followed him to the buggy. "What's going on?"

"Nothing," Daniel quickly said as he took the reins, but she knew he was lying.

"Daniel?" Ruby asked again, this time in a persistent tone of voice.

Daniel just laughed, "Wait and see."

The rest of the ride into town was quiet. As they approached the bakery, Ruby saw dozens of people gathered outside. "Oh my gosh, did something happen?"

Daniel shook his head, "*Nee,* but it's about to."

Ruby followed him to the entrance of the store and noticed even the newspaper man was there. "Daniel... what's going on?"

Daniel smiled before turning to the crowd. "As promised, we're on time, and the lady we're celebrating today is standing right beside me." Daniel nodded to someone standing by the door and suddenly a cloth dropped from the awning.

Ruby turned and gasped as she saw all that was unfolding.

The green awning that read Fischer's Amish bakery was now pink and the name had changed to…

Ruby's.

A tear slipped from her eye as she turned to her husband. "Daniel?"

"You're the reason I get up in the morning. I can't think of a better way to spend my day than with Ruby."

The words were sweet and Ruby wanted to take a moment to drink it all in but that wasn't possible.

"Daniel?" Ruby said a little nervously.

*"Jah?"* Daniel asked with a broad smile.

"I know you've gone to a lot of trouble and I can see everyone's expecting the bakery to open, but we've got to be somewhere else," Ruby spoke through clenched teeth as she clasped her swollen belly.

"We're exactly where we need to be," Daniel said reassuringly.

*"Nee,* we're not. We need to be at the hospital because your *boppli* decided to be a part of this special day."

Daniel laughed and before the laughter faded, surprised dawned on his face. "Now?"

"Now!" Ruby said with a nod.

The crowd parted as Daniel moved beside Ruby. Today was going to be a day they'd never forget.

## Chapter Twenty

Ruby felt Daniel's strong hand clasp over hers as the strong pains of labor made her knees tremble. She couldn't believe it was happening now. For the last week she had stayed at home to wait for her boppli to be born.

It was supposed to be special moment. A moment that she would never forget, and when her water broke as she looked up at the beautiful sign bearing her name, she knew she never would. It was as if even their unborn child wanted a part in their happiness. The happiness Ruby didn't believe she would ever experience after what happened with her first engagement.

As for Jacob, no one had heard of him since the summer before. Ruby prayed he found happiness but in her heart she knew she had chosen the right husband. How could she have married a man who would believe a rumor over the word of his own fiancée?

A laugh escaped Ruby as Daniel rushed her to the buggy. "Are you sure it's happening?"

"Daniel, when your body feels like it's twisting in two and you can barely walk…it's happening!"

She watched the fear wash over his face before it was

replaced with excitement. Today their happy ending would get the icing on the cake, just like the beautiful cakes Ruby baked for the bakery. She let Daniel help her into the buggy and as soon as she was seated, she thought of her family back home in Lancaster.

When she had come to Ohio to visit, she had never imagined that she wouldn't return to Lancaster County, but Ohio was her home now.

Millersburg and Daniel were her home.

Another pain grabbed hold of her abdomen, pulling it taut with treacherous bands as Ruby tried to breathe through the pain like the other young mothers had advised her. But the breathing didn't help for the pain, and the buggy's bouncing gait only made it worse.

Her parents, David and Anna King, were elated at the thought of their first grandchild's arrival and Ruby couldn't wait to see them when they came to meet their grandchild. As for Mary, although she had apologized for her interference in Ruby's engagement to Jacob by sewing Ruby's wedding dress, things had never been the same between them. Weeks, sometimes months would go by before her sister answered her letters.

Although her parents assured her that her sister was happily courting, it bothered Ruby that the relationship between her and her sister had never recovered. Others might bear grudges for months or even years over what Mary had done, but in the end, Ruby realized her sister had done it out of love.

"Are you alright?" Daniel asked holding the reins, concern shining in his eyes.

Ruby forced out a laugh for the sake of his concern. "Women have been giving birth for centuries, I'll be fine."

Even though the words tripped off her tongue like they were the truth, Ruby couldn't help but wonder if the pain was supposed to be this bad. Her hands protectively wrapped over her abdomen, she kept her eyes on the horizon, wishing for the hospital to come into sight.

Her thoughts trailed back to her family and for a brief moment she wished they were here. What she wouldn't give to have her mother by her side right now. How many times had her mother told her and Mary that you only appreciated your mother once you became one? Ruby understood those words too well right now.

Another contraction took hold of her body, this one worse than the one before. Ruby gasped and screwed her eyes shut, counting the seconds, when Daniel suddenly took her hand. "Ruby, you're pale as a ghost, are you sure you're fine?"

She nodded, unable to speak but smiling through the pain. "I think this little one is in a hurry."

Daniel laughed, "I can't wait to meet him or her."

"Have you thought of a name yet?" Ruby asked trying to put him at ease although they had chosen names a few weeks back.

"*Jah*, I think we should stick with what we said. Elizabeth if it's a girl and David if it's a boy."

"My *daed* would be so pleased to have his grandson named after him."

"I'm sure. Here we are." Daniel smiled as he pulled the buggy up to the emergency entrance.

Ruby took a deep breath and let it out through her mouth. She just needed to make it into the hospital, and everything would be fine, she assured herself. She waited for Daniel to come around and help her out of the buggy. "Let's go have a *boppli*."

Excitement rippled in the air as Daniel helped her towards the doors.

## Chapter Twenty-One

The following morning Daniel's eyes were dry and scratchy; his heart ached in his chest as he glanced down at a sleeping Ruby. Everything had gone as planned when they arrived at hospital. He'd never seen anyone as brave as Ruby in labor. Not once did she complain or ask for something for the pain. She held onto his hand and prayed quietly until their son was born.

David Fischer had been born only an hour after their arrival at hospital. But the excitement was short lived.

As soon as the nurses took the baby to clean and weigh him, the machines in the room began sounding a deafening alarm. Two nurses rushed out of the room with his baby as four more rushed in to help the doctor. Daniel was asked to leave although he didn't understand what was happening. All he knew was that something was very very wrong. More doctors arrived as Daniel stood in the hallway.

He couldn't remember ever feeling as lost in his life. The nurses had taken the baby into care while Ruby was fighting for her life. He had dropped down against the stark white hospital wall and prayed for God to be with her. It took almost an hour before a doctor came to talk to him.

An hour before he learned that the birth of their son had almost cost Ruby her life. Hemorrhaging wasn't uncommon during labor, but it was also not common. Especially not the severe hemorrhaging that Ruby had suffered. Instead of being moved to the maternity ward to recuperate after the birth and to bond with her child, Ruby had been moved to intensive care while the neo-natal nurses cared for baby David.

Daniel hadn't moved from her side except for the brief time it had taken him to send word to Lancaster of the birth and the complications. He knew Ruby's parents would already be on their way but he couldn't stand the thought of leaving her side.

She had swept into his life and his bakery like a breath of fresh air. He had fallen for her hard and fast and had built an entire life of dreams around their love. The entire night Daniel had kept watch over her. There were so many machines and tubes attached; Daniel wouldn't know where to start explaining which machine did what exactly. He cared only that they had brought her through the night. Surely the first night was the most vital for her survival?

The maternity nurse had fetched him to meet his son, but Daniel had once again declined. He wouldn't meet his son before Ruby had the honor. She had carried him for nine months and it was her privilege to meet her son first. Besides, Daniel couldn't stand the thought of stepping away for just a minute, what if something happened while he was gone?

When the doctor came to check on Ruby, Daniel was certain the prognosis would be positive. Instead the doctor explained the dire complications caused by the hemorrhage. They had managed to subdue it the night before but it still hadn't stopped. Before Daniel could try to understand what the doctor meant, Ruby was rushed back into surgery.

It was like the nightmare that wouldn't stop.

Ruby's parents arrived before she was out of surgery. Although Daniel explained what had happened, they were just as surprised as Daniel at how soon things had turned.

Together they bowed their heads in prayer, waiting for the doctor to bring them news.

Late that afternoon the doctor finally returned to the room to find three pairs of eyes pleading for good news.

"I can see you're all very concerned. The operation went well; we managed to staunch the hemorrhage completely although there were a few complications…"

Before the doctor could continue Daniel stood up and took a few steps towards him. "Is she alright?"

The doctor nodded. "She will be. Her recovery might take some time and due to the surgery and the medication, she won't be able to breastfeed, but in time she will recover perfectly."

A symphony of sighs sounded through the room as Anna King rushed into her husband's arms. Daniel sighed gratefully and cast his eyes to the roof to thank God for being with her during this trying time. "And my son?"

"Your son is also doing fine. The nurses in neo are taking perfectly good care of him. You're welcome to visit with him."

"*Nee*, not until I'm sure that Ruby is fine."

"Daniel, you should go. Your *seeh* needs you." Anna

stepped forward and placed an encouraging hand on his shoulder.

Daniel shook his head. "You should go, your grandson needs you. I need my wife." His voice broke but he quickly swallowed back the tears.

His parents in law looked at him with sympathy in their eyes. "We'll go take care of David; you wait here for Ruby to come out of recovery."

Daniel nodded, grateful that they understood he needed to be with Ruby. He waited for almost thirty minutes before her bed was finally wheeled back into the room. If she had looked pale this morning, she now reminded him of a porcelain doll. Her skin was devoid of color, her eyes closed in a drugged sleep. His beautiful, vibrant wife looked as if she had already left this world for the next; all that told him differently was the heart rate monitor that beeped at a slow pace.

Daniel took her hand in his; it was small and limp as he pressed a kiss to it. "Please my dear Ruby, don't leave me now. We have so much we still want to share; you still have to meet our beautiful *seeh*."

She didn't respond, Daniel didn't expect her to.

All he expected was for her to recover and come home to help him raise their son.

# Chapter Twenty-Two

*Six months later...*

Mary King, now Mary Zook, glanced down at her swollen belly and smiled. So much had happened in the last two years, so much to be ashamed of, to feel guilty for, to repent about and yet God had blessed her with a husband and the life growing inside her.

She glanced out the window of her small two bedroom home and sighed contently as her baby kicked inside her. With the rolling hills of Lancaster County dotting the landscape in the distance, she thought of Ruby.

Six months ago when David was born, Ruby had almost died. During those few weeks that Ruby had spent in hospital recovering, Mary had packed and unpacked her bags almost ten times to see her sister, but in the end, she had never taken the bus to Ohio.

Although Ruby had forgiven her on the day of her wedding to Daniel Fischer, Mary had yet to forgive herself for what she had done.

In her heart she believed that Ruby and Daniel belonged together but that didn't mean that causing her sister heartache and ruining her engagement to Jacob had been a kind deed. No, it had been an awful thing to do, and Mary would regret it for the rest of her life. She had let jealousy cloud her mind and determine her actions; actions that had hurt her sister more than she could ever imagine and had caused Jacob to leave the community.

She could still remember the devastated expression on his face when he had found out that she had lied merely for her own benefit.

A heavy sighed escaped her as a tear whispered down her cheek. She had managed to put aside that time in her life for so long. She had found a wonderful husband who loved her more than she ever deserved. Caleb Zook had started courting her shortly before Ruby's wedding. At first Mary had tried to refuse his affections, but it had soon become clear that Caleb was as determined about courting her as he was about farming.

Slowly he had managed to break down her defenses until she one day broke down and told him why she didn't deserve love. The wonderful man that he was, Caleb had taken her in his arms and told her that everyone made mistakes, but loving him wouldn't be one.

Her resolve had softened and she had fallen in love. On their wedding day Ruby had stood amongst her family and smiled warmly at her. After the ceremony she had wished her sister every blessing that God could give and yet Mary still doubted she deserved any of it.

After all she had done to her sister, the shame she had brought to her parents, Mary couldn't seem to find that love or forgiveness for herself. Of course she tried to move on with her life. She and Caleb had married, and she had left her own congregation to join his, she wouldn't admit that it suited her not to see her parents at every church Sunday.

The new congregation had given her a chance at starting afresh. Here no one knew of the vile rumors she had spread about her sister and no one knew of the guilt and the blame she carried inside her. One day, she promised herself, she would try to forgive herself, but until that day it was best she didn't see her family as often as they wished.

When Ruby, Daniel and their newborn son, David, had come to the wedding, it had pained Mary to see her sister so pale and wan. After the complications of birth, it had taken Ruby almost a month to recover in hospital before she could go home. Their little boy was a true darling, all gummy smiles and giggles and yet Mary knew she didn't deserve to be a part of his life. She had thanked her sister for coming all the way for the wedding, but she hadn't truly spent time with her or tried to mend what had been broken.

Every time she saw her sister or her parents, she was reminded of the horrible thing she had done. To drive her sister to Ohio with her bad deeds had been the worst punishment of all. Although she had always been jealous of Ruby, she had loved her dearly.

She missed them doing everything together, the way they had finished each other's sentences, but Mary knew it would never be that way between them again.

Because of her.

She brushed the tears away when she noticed Caleb approaching from his carpentry shed behind the house.

"There she is," Caleb said, closing the kitchen door behind him. "Day dreaming?"

Mary nodded with a smile. Often when she stood thinking about her family and what she had done, Caleb thought she was daydreaming. If only he knew that to her it felt more like reliving a nightmare.

"Just thinking about the *boppli*."

"Crib is almost finished. Now I just need to get started on the rocking chair."

"But we have rocking chairs," Mary chuckled. "Five of them."

Caleb shook his head as he wrapped his arms around her waist. "You need a nursing chair. One that will be used for all our *kinners*, one that will one day remind us of this special time and the purpose for which it was built."

"What did I do to deserve you?" Mary asked leaning back against his shoulder. How many times could she thank God for the wonderful man he had given her?

"Absolutely nothing, because you deserve only the best."

As if the baby agreed it, kicked at that moment bringing a smile to Mary's face. Although her eyes were filled with sorrow because in her heart she knew she didn't deserve anything at all.

# Chapter Twenty-Three

At the very moment Mary's hand caressed her swollen belly, Ruby and Daniel sat in the doctor's office in Ohio.

"Relax," Daniel squeezed Ruby's hand. "I'm sure everything will be fine."

Ruby wanted to believe him. She so badly wanted everything to be fine, but after the nightmare of David's birth, Ruby was careful about positive assumptions. Although her bouncing baby boy was healthy, his life had almost cost Ruby hers. She had lost the first few weeks of her baby's life to doctors and hospitals while she fought with all her courage for her life.

She didn't remember much about the birth, only the terrible pain and the darkness that enveloped her before she heard her son's first cries as he struggled his way into the world.

At six months, David was the happiest baby. He smiled at everyone and gurgled playfully whenever Ruby or Daniel picked him up. They had truly been blessed with a beautiful child, which was their reason for sitting in the doctor's office today.

When Ruby was released from hospital five months

ago, the doctor had given her strict instructions to come for a checkup when David was six months old. At first Ruby had believed the check up was just routine, but as time passed and she spoke to other mothers, she realized there was nothing routine about seeing a specialist six months after your baby's birth. Six weeks perhaps, but not six months.

The door squeaked open and the doctor walked into the room with a tentative smile. "Ruby, Daniel, it's good to see you again. I see you've gained some weight, Ruby, and the color has returned to your cheeks. You had me apprehensive there for quite some time."

Ruby smiled as nerves made her fingers tremble in Daniel's hand. "*Denke* for everything you did, Doctor. I truly appreciate it."

"My pleasure. You're probably wondering why I asked you to come and see me." The doctor took a seat behind his desk as he opened what Ruby assumed was her file."

"*Jah*, I must admit we were a bit concerned as well," Daniel glanced at Ruby before turning back to the doctor.

The doctor nodded. "I can understand that. I wanted to give you some time with your son before we had this conversation. Were you planning on having more children?"

Ruby smiled at Daniel before looking at the doctor. "*Jah*, we're planning on having a large *familye*, but I think I'll wait a year or two before I have the courage to have another child." A nervous chuckle escaped her but it quickly faded when she noticed the doctor's somber expression.

He let out a heavy sigh. "Ruby, after the birth I explained to Daniel that we're going to do everything we can to save your life. We did, which I'm grateful for, but in the process, we might have impeded your chances of having children. That's why I asked you to come in. I'd like to run a couple of tests and scans just to see how your uterus has recovered after the hemorrhage and the operation. Once we have all the results we can approach the future with a clearer idea of what's going on."

Ruby frowned, "But you didn't give me a hysterectomy, surely that means I can still bear children."

The doctor took off his glasses and looked at Ruby with a concerned gaze. "Ruby, let's do the tests and see what happens. It doesn't help to jump to conclusions before we have the results."

Ruby spent the rest of the day at the hospital. The blood work would be sent to the doctor once the results were in, but the doctor would give them the results of the scan today. With Daniel at her side they returned to the doctor's rooms after the scan. Before he opened the door, Daniel turned to her with a smile. "It doesn't matter what happens now, we have each other, Ruby."

Ruby smiled, knowing he was right.

They walked inside and took a seat but Ruby didn't miss the defeated expression on the doctor's face as he closed the file in front of him. "Thanks for coming back. I've got the results of your scan."

"And?" Daniel asked, sitting forward in his seat.

"I was afraid this would happen," the doctor sighed heavily and shook his head. "Sometimes when there is a hemorrhage during birth, especially when it's a severe one like the one Ruby suffered, we need to cauterize the bleeding to save a life. In Ruby's case we managed to save her life but her uterus isn't what it used to be. The scarring, although healed, is quite severe. I'm afraid having more children could put Ruby and the child's life at risk. With a scarred uterus, the chances of carrying to term are very slim and even if she does carry to term, labor contractions could cause the uterus to rupture and claim both Ruby's and the baby's lives."

Ruby listened with her eyes closed as the doctor explained how she would never be able to have another child. She didn't even open her eyes as the first tear slipped over her cheek. She knew she had to be grateful for David, that they'd both survived what could have turned out to be fatal, but how she had yearned for a little girl.

Ruby stood up, oblivious to Daniel's concerned look or the apology in the doctor's eyes.

"*Denke* for your trouble, Doctor. Have a *gut* day." Even in a moment of personal turmoil and inadequacy at being unable to give Daniel the children he deserved; she kept her smile in place as she walked to the door.

She heard Daniel and the doctor exchange a few brief words as she opened the door and walked out. She would not dwell on this, she promised herself. God had blessed her with David and although she would never bear another child, she would give David all the love she had to give.

Daniel's hastened footsteps sounded through the passage as she raced towards her. "Ruby, wait! Are you alright?"

She turned to her husband with a smile in place. "*Nee*, I'm not, but we have David and we have our faith—I will be eventually."

She knew the news was just as earth shattering to him as it was to her, but right now all she could think of was fetching her son from the neighbor and holding his small body against hers, and to be grateful for having him instead of being furious that she wouldn't have any more babies.

## Chapter Twenty-Four

A week after their visit to the doctor's office Ruby couldn't seem to accept the fact that she would bear no more children.

She was more than grateful that she had little David, but after dreaming of one day having a large family it was as if she was mourning the loss of that dream. She could see it bothered Daniel as well, although he didn't mention it.

It was Saturday morning and Daniel had just returned from the bakery to find Ruby outside hanging out the laundry. The sun was shining down, teasing the flowers to bloom but Ruby's heart felt as if a thunder cloud had settled over it indefinitely.

David was down for his nap when Ruby saw the buggy approach and she couldn't help but wish that Daniel had remained at the bakery a little longer. Not because she didn't want to see him, but because she couldn't stand the thought of him seeing her when she was so sad.

He crossed the yard towards her with a bright smile.

"Nothing like the scent of laundry detergent in the breeze. How was your morning?"

Ruby smiled, although she knew it didn't reach her eyes. "David's been busy, but otherwise just a regular Saturday morning."

A frown creased Daniel's brow. "Ruby, I can see it's bothering you. *Kumm*, let's go sit on the porch and talk about this."

Ruby quickly shook her head. "It's no use. What will talking do? Talking won't heal my uterus, talking won't give you the *kinners* you dreamed of."

Daniel stepped back in surprise. "The *kinners* we dreamed of."

Ruby could see the pain in his gaze and hated that she had just turned her anger on him. "I'm sorry; I'm just so sad and angry. Angry that this happened. Angry that I can't change it. Angry that I'll never be able to have more *bopplin*. That David will never have a *bruder* or a *schweschder*."

Daniel slowly stepped forward and took the basket from Ruby's hand. "*Kumm*, we're going to talk about this before you explode with anger and sorrow."

Before Ruby could argue, Daniel led her up the porch. She hated that he could be this reasonable in the face of such an impossible situation, but she knew later that evening she would appreciate it.

"Ruby, I know this isn't the life we planned. I know we wanted a boisterous *familye* and sibling fights, but I'm sure *Gott* has a reason. We were blessed with David when I could have lost you both. I'm not angry, I'm not even angry at the doctor for not telling us straight away. I'm just grateful he saved your life."

"I know." Ruby sighed heavily. "I just wish… I don't know how to accept this."

"Have you spoken to your mother or a friend, perhaps?" Daniel asked gently.

Ruby shook her head. "I don't want to talk to my *mamm* about this. She'll just be reasonable, like you." Ruby smiled sadly at Daniel before she continued. "The person I wish I could talk to isn't answering my letters."

Daniel sighed heavily. "She still hasn't replied?"

*"Nee."* Ruby sighed shaking her head. "I write to her almost every week and she doesn't even reply. I need her, Daniel. I used to be able to share everything with her and now she won't even reply to my letters."

"Write to her, tell her what's happened. Perhaps, if she realizes you need her, she'll write back."

Ruby nodded although she knew that wasn't the answer. How could she share such personal news with her sister when her sister wouldn't even share every day news with her? "I'll think about it."

"Just remember, Ruby, we're blessed more than most. Let's count our blessings. We have David and he's the biggest blessing of all. Mary will come around. Perhaps now that she's married… I'm sure she'll realize she needs you just as much."

Ruby couldn't help but sigh. Mary had never needed anyone. She had always been self-sufficient. She had always been the one who could do anything and everything without any support. Ruby had never realized how much she had depended on her sister until she moved to Ohio. Mary's betrayal had created a rift between them and although Ruby had put it in the past and forgiven Mary, it was as if the rift had become a canyon she would never be able to cross.

"Come on, let's go check on David," Ruby said as she began to stand up, but Daniel drew her back.

"First promise me you'll talk to me when you're sad. I know how hard this has been on you but I don't want you to feel guilty. It isn't your fault and I don't care that we can't have more *kinners*, as long as I have you and David."

Ruby smiled up at her husband's loving gaze. How could she have ever mistaken the childhood affection she felt for Jacob for real love. What she felt for Daniel was so much more. It was a love that could endure the hard times, that could celebrate the good times; a love that could celebrate in everyday tasks as ordinary as cooking together.

"I promise I'll talk to you. I know we'll get through this, I just… I feel like a failure somehow."

Daniel clucked his tongue. "You're an excellent baker, a wonderful *mamm* and a good wife. How could you fail us?"

Feeling the clouds fade away, Ruby smiled up at her husband. "Only a good wife but an excellent baker? Remind me not to iron your shirts anymore."

Daniel laughed, "You're a magnificent wife. No other wife would set out my clothes every morning."

Ruby smiled. "And no other husband would name his bakery after his wife."

They headed inside but Ruby couldn't help but wonder if she shouldn't consider sharing her bad news with Mary. She quickly shoved the thought aside and reminded herself they no longer shared that close bond. This was something she would work through on her own and lean on her husband when she felt she couldn't carry the burden alone.

## Chapter Twenty-Five

The months seemed to fly by while Mary and Caleb prepared for the arrival of their first child. The crib was the most beautiful piece of furniture she had ever seen and the rocking chair that matched it was just as breathtaking.

The letters that kept coming from Ohio were stacked in a cake tin in the kitchen. Mary knew she needed to write to her sister, she needed to forgive herself since her sister had forgiven her a long time ago, but she couldn't help the guilt and shame that washed over her each time she read her sister's words.

Their little boy, David, named after their father, was clearly the light and love of Ruby's life. Mary knew it would only be a matter of time before news of their second baby would arrive. She wished her sister every happiness in the world although she felt guilty for taking that happiness for herself. From the frequent letters it was clear that Ruby had fully recovered after the traumatic month following David's birth. Mary couldn't help but fear the same complications with her own child.

Every night when the house grew quiet with Caleb

quietly snoring beside her, she prayed for God to be with her and the baby when the time came.

In her swollen belly the space had grown a little taut. In place of the bountiful kicks she felt a month ago, these days it felt more like nudges to try and make more space.

Sleeping had become a luxury that Mary rarely experienced soundly; she was as big as she was uncomfortable and although she knew that every day could be the day her baby made its arrival, she hoped it would be soon. Caleb had taken to working around the house more often, wanting to be close by when Mary needed him, although she was certain she would be able to summon the midwife on her own when the time came.

Most of her friends had opted to birth their children in hospital, but Mary had dreamed of a homebirth. The nursery was ready, the pantry stocked and all the preparations for the arrival of their baby made. But it seemed her baby was in no hurry at all.

The sun had yet to make its ascent over the eastern hills, but the first beams of light had already reached Lancaster County. Mary shifted in bed, flinching when a sharp stabbing pain shot through her abdomen. Clasping her bump with both hands, she breathed until the pain subsided. Her baby was probably just trying to carve out a little space for himself, she reasoned as she headed to the kitchen to brew coffee for Caleb.

When the second pain clenched her like a tight-fisted band, she still reasoned it away. She busied herself by making coffee and preparing breakfast when the third pain clamped like a vice around her waist. This time she couldn't catch her breath. She counted back from ten, trying to summon her voice to call out to Caleb, but it was no use. The pain was more excruciating than she had ever imagined.

She let out a grateful sigh when she heard Caleb's footsteps behind her as she leaned her weight over a chair.

"Mary?" his voice was filled with concern. "Is it time?"

Mary could do no more than nod as another pain struck her. Caleb pressed a kiss to her forehead before rushing out of the house. He was going to summon the midwife.

What had started at dawn ended at sunset. A day of breathing through the pain, trying to find courage to take another breath just to be struck down by more pain, finally resulted in the cries of her baby girl sounding through the house.

Ella Zook was born at sunset, weighing in at a healthy seven pounds and eight ounces. Her blue newborn gaze made Mary's heart swell as she looked at her daughter's face. Ella was perfect with ten fingers, ten toes, her mother's mouth and her father's nose. Once the midwife was certain that Mary didn't need further care and that the baby was feeding, she left the new parents to revel in the arrival of their first child.

With Caleb at her side and Ella in her arms, a tear slipped down Mary's cheek. She knew this moment was sacred; it was a moment for family. Their first moment as a family, but she couldn't help but wish that her parents and Ruby had been there to share it with her.

"She's beautiful, Mary, truly a little angel."

Mary smiled up at her husband. "Of all the things I've done wrong in this life, I must have done something right for *Gott* to have given me a little angel."

"Would you like me to send word to your parents?" Caleb asked brushing a gentle thumb over Ella's cheek.

Mary nodded, "*Jah, denke*. They're going to be elated. And Caleb…could you bring me a sheet of paper and a pen? I'd like to write to Ruby."

Caleb's eyes widened, surprised, "Are you sure?"

"*Jah*, it's time to put the past behind us. I'd like Ella to know her cousin and I'd like to see more of my *schweschder*."

Caleb smiled knowing what a big moment this was for Mary. "I'll be back in a minute."

## Chapter Twenty-Six

Ruby placed David on the seat of the buggy. He was almost eighteen months old and although he was still just her baby boy, he was becoming more of a boy than a baby with every passing day.

"Are we going to visit *Daed*?" Ruby asked with a broad smile as she climbed up and took the reins. The doctor's prognosis more than a year ago still caused a lingering ache in her heart, but she wouldn't allow that ache to detract from what she had with her little boy. The yearning for more children had never left her and although she and Daniel never discussed it again, she knew it affected him similarly.

It was as if they both refused to acknowledge that conversation. While they pretended it had never taken place, there was still hope and neither was ready to give up on hope just yet.

Ruby led the horse down the dirt drive and stopped at the mailbox. They rarely received mail, and the only mail she truly wished for never came.

Mail from her beloved sister.

She made sure David was still seated before she

climbed out to check the mailbox and found three en-
velopes. The first was a bill from David's doctor for
his check up the month before; the second was a letter
from her mother that brought a smile to her face; the
third caused her smile to fade.

She rushed back to the buggy and climbed up before tearing at the envelope. She had written to Mary
almost every fortnight since her move to Ohio but had
not once received a letter in return. She unfolded the
paper and eagerly lapped up the words.

*My dearest schweschder*

*Denke for your continuous letters. I'm grateful
you have recovered and wish you and Daniel only
blessings with your next boppli.*

*I write this letter with a light heart and a smile
to inform you of my dochder's birth. Ella Zook
was born on the fifth of June at sunset, without
complications.*
*Congratulations on becoming an aunt.*

*Love,*
*Mary*

A frown creased Ruby's brow as she read the letter
over and over again. When she wrote to her sister, her
letters were filled with tidbits about her life, memories
from their childhood and news on David and Daniel.

She appreciated the letter from her sister as well
as her kind words and blessings, but five sentences?
She might as well have been a complete stranger. Ruby
sighed heavily as she folded the letter and placed it back

in the envelope. It seemed it didn't matter how hard Ruby tried to repair the bond between them, Mary simply wasn't interested.

It was as if the sister who had once been her best friend was now a distant relative who would only write when there was news of a birth or death. The thought was so depressing that Ruby pushed it to the back of her mind.

She couldn't help but remember the last letter from her mother which had mentioned how distant Mary had become. Was this because of Caleb? *Nee.* Ruby pushed that thought aside as well. Mary had always been her own person. If she wasn't writing, it was because she didn't want to. There wasn't a single excuse that made sense for her sister's reticence to be a part of their lives; maybe it was time Ruby accepted that Mary didn't want them to be as close as they once were.

A tear slipped over her cheek as she took the reins. Instead of going to Ruby's Bakery, she headed straight to her Aunt Elizabeth.

Elizabeth had been the shoulder she had cried on after losing Jacob and although Ruby had found love since then, Aunt Elizabeth was still the best friend she had in Millersburg. Had it not been for Elizabeth's encouragement, Ruby would have never taken her cakes to Fischer's Bakery and she would never have met Daniel. Her aunt was instrumental in her happiness and Ruby knew she would have some answers for her now.

Elizabeth was sitting on her porch when Ruby arrived. "Ruby dear, what a *gut* surprise. I was just about to make tea."

Elizabeth scooped David from Ruby's arms. "You're becoming such a big boy."

One look at Ruby and her smile faded. "What's happened, Ruby? You look troubled."

Ruby shrugged, "Mary wrote."

"That's *wunderbaar*," Elizabeth said before a frown creased her brow. "Why don't you look happy then? You've been waiting for her to write you for years."

Ruby swallowed back the disappointment and nodded. "*Jah*, but when she finally did, I didn't expect to feel like a stranger she felt obliged to tell about the birth of her *dochder*."

"You're an aunt? Congratulations, Ruby. Why do you say you felt like a stranger?"

Ruby helped David down the steps to chase a butterfly on the lawn and handed the letter to Elizabeth. After a few seconds, she looked at Ruby with a frown of her own, "She might have just been in a hurry or…ach Ruby, I'm so sorry. I don't know what to say about this."

"Neither do I," Ruby admitted ruefully. "I thought after my wedding, after hers…that things would finally be the way they were again, but it seems she doesn't even care to try and revive the friendship we once had."

"I don't know your *schweschder* very well and I don't know why she did what she did back then, but I do know that giving birth takes a lot out of a woman. Give her time, perhaps she's just a little overwhelmed. A little girl…" Elizabeth's smile broadened. "Can you imagine that? A little cousin for David. You have to take him to meet her."

Ruby tilted her head. She had thought the same, but Mary had never taken the trouble to meet her son. Why should she go to the trouble when her sister's letter had just made the distance between them clear? "Maybe, maybe when we go see *Mamm* and *Daed* again."

Elizabeth drew Ruby into a hug before drawing back and smiling. "Remember, blood is thicker than water. She might have forgotten that but she'll remember it soon enough."

Ruby smiled but she couldn't help but wonder if just this once Elizabeth was wrong. She didn't know what else she could do to restore the friendship she had with her sister. How could she let Mary realize that she loved her and needed her if her sister felt intent on shutting her out of her life.

She visited with Elizabeth for quite a while before she headed home. She shared the news with Daniel and yet the dark cloud wouldn't seem to lift. When she went to bed she prayed for guidance, hoping God would have the answers she couldn't seem to find.

*Gott, please help me repair what's broken between me and Mary. I love her so much and I miss her but it's as if she's treating me as if I did something to wrong her. Please Gott, open her heart to my love and friendship and let us again be the schweschders we once were. I pray of you, Gott, to guard her new little girl and let us put the past behind us so our kinners can grow up like the cousins they truly are.*

## Chapter Twenty-Seven

Over the weeks that followed, Ruby couldn't seem to forget about the letter from Mary. It bothered her on a level that made her wonder if her sister still loved her. She had thought back to Mary's wedding and realized that, except for a brief hello and thank you for coming, Mary had avoided her for the rest of the day.

In her mind she had placated herself over the years by thinking Mary simply wasn't one who enjoyed writing. Now, late at night, that thought seemed to bring her peace, but in the bright light of day it was hard to accept that her sister just didn't care about her anymore.

The anger she had buried on the day of her wedding over all her sister had done, had reemerged with such fury that she struggled to get through a day without remembering it.

One evening after dinner when David was already put down for the night, Ruby took her cup of tea out on the porch. Daniel, who knew her better than she knew herself, joined her outside, taking a seat in the rocker beside her. Without saying a word he took her hand and sat in silence for a full half hour before finally turning to her with a concerned look. "This is still about that letter from your *schweschder, jah*?"

A heavy sigh escaped Ruby as she squeezed her husband's hand. "I can't stop thinking about it. I'm the one who should have been distancing myself from her after what she did, not the other way around."

Daniel nodded thoughtfully before he turned to Ruby. "I've never asked, since it happened before I met you. But what exactly happened? All I know is that she somehow ended your engagement with Jacob."

Ruby sighed heavily. She had tried to forget what had caused the rift between her and Mary for such a long time, but it was only fair that Daniel knew. "Since I could remember, Mary, Jacob and I were best friends. We did everything together. He was like the *bruder* we never had. Until one day my *mamm* announced that an arrangement had been made for me and Jacob to wed once we were baptized."

Daniel cocked a brow. "An arranged marriage? Sounds a little archaic to me."

Ruby shrugged with a sad smile. "It probably was, but we were such *gut* friends, I didn't mind."

"What happened then?" Daniel asked when Ruby got lost in thought for a moment.

"I'm not really sure. I don't remember Mary being upset about it, although I guess we both expected a match would be made for her first. Jacob and I tried to keep including Mary in our adventures, but she seemed to draw back. In time, it was just me and Jacob."

"And Mary had withdrawn herself completely?"

"Exactly. I thought we were falling in love as we began to plan our future together. We were best friends and we knew each other's stories. It felt right, you know?" Ruby sighed and shook her head. "Until one day I got a letter from him saying that he was done being a puppet in my puppet show. He broke off the engagement without further explanation. I was shattered; but if I think back now, it was more because I didn't know who I would be if I wasn't with Jacob, if you understand?"

"Your whole life had revolved around him and now that he was no longer there, you felt lost?"

"*Jah*. I came to Ohio to clear my mind and met and fell in love with you. While that was happening it turned out that Mary had spread lies about me to Jacob."

"Hoping that he would love her instead?" Daniel nodded beginning to understand.

"*Jah*, but he didn't. When he found out she had told him lies, he left the community. No one knows where he's gone."

"Poor *mann* was probably devastated."

"He was, but now I can't imagine being with him instead of you. It's as if it happened for a reason. I've forgiven her long ago, but still things between us aren't right."

"So you've forgiven her, but now she's the one still giving you the cold shoulder?" Daniel shook his head.

"*Jah*, exactly. I promised myself I would forgive her and put the past behind me, but this letter makes me wonder if I should have forgiven her at all. I know now it was done out of jealousy, that it was done because she loved Jacob, but why should I try to heal our relationship when it's clear she still doesn't care about me?"

"I'm sure she cares about you. I'm also sure she has her reasons. Sometimes another's heart is as murky as stagnant water."

"I know, but Daniel, she's got her own husband now, her own *kind*. Surely since she's found love, she's realized that what happened with Jacob years ago doesn't matter anymore."

"Have you told her that?" Daniel asked carefully.

Ruby frowned. "How do you mean?"

"Have you explicitly told her you love her and that you want to be friends again, as you once were?"

"*Nee*, but surely it could have been inferred when we attended the wedding."

"Just like she could have inferred that you attended the wedding out of respect and not because you have forgiven her."

Ruby frowned and realized her husband might be right. "*Jah*, that might be true. Ach Daniel, it's just hard for me to accept that she tried to ruin my happiness all those years ago and that now I'm the one begging for her to be a part of my life. I didn't think it would be this way."

"We hardly ever know which way it's going to be. Pray for her to let you into her life again, Ruby, and don't give up. Keep writing and maybe you should consider going to visit her."

"But what about you?" Ruby asked as her heart swelled with love for the generous man in front of her. A trip to Ohio wasn't worth the expense if it wasn't at least for a month or two.

"I'll be *gut* here. I took care of myself for a long time before I met you. Besides, it would give David a chance to play with his baby cousin and get to know your parents a little better."

Ruby considered it for a moment. It sounded like a wonderful plan. She could stay with her parents and mend fences with Mary, but ultimately, she didn't think it would be worth it. If Mary didn't even bother to write a proper letter, why would she bother to welcome her sister into her home?

"I'll think about it. *Denke* for listening."

"I might not be much of a talker, but I've always had broad shoulders," Daniel said, wrapping an arm around her shoulders. "Have I told you today that I love you?"

Ruby laughed, "Not yet."

## Chapter Twenty-Eight

Whenever she looked into Ella's eyes, Mary couldn't stop the guilt from washing over her. It was as if her daughter was a reminder of what she had done to her own sister. Was Ruby truly happy or would she have been happier if Mary hadn't interfered in her relationship with Jacob? Would Ruby have gone to Ohio if it hadn't been for her foul rumors?

It was as if the what-ifs kept piling up as the months passed after Ella's birth. Every letter she received from her sister made her feel guiltier, more inadequate about caring for her daughter.

How could someone who betrayed her own sister provide a loving home for a little girl? What kind of example would she set for Ella? Would Ella also be capable of the same jealousy that had made Mary do the unthinkable to end her sister's engagement?

Ella was the light in her and Caleb's life. Ella brought happiness, joy and love into their home and Mary couldn't help but feel as if she didn't deserve any of it. Over the last few weeks, Caleb had asked her more than once about the reason behind the darkness in her eyes, but Mary couldn't tell him. How could she tell her husband that she didn't think she was a good mother, or that she didn't deserve their beautiful little girl?

Once, long ago, the bishop had preached about sins catching up with us. Mary often wondered if the guilt and the shame was God's way of punishing her for what she had done. She prayed for release from the guilt and yet she couldn't seem to let it go.

It was a cool winter's evening when the postman dropped a letter in her mailbox. She didn't have to guess who the letter was from. She wrapped her coat tightly around her and retrieved the envelope from the mailbox. Over a cup of tea she read the words her sister had written.

*My dear schweschder,*

*I miss the days we would play in the stream and talk about everything and anything. I miss the days we couldn't seem to stop talking. Where every secret, every event had to be shared.*

*What happened to those days?*

*Denke for your letter, and congratulations on the birth of your little girl. I can't wait to meet her. If I'm welcome, I'd love to come and see her soon.*

*I love you, Mary, and in my heart I know it's simply a matter of time before we share everything again. Please don't draw further away than you already have. Distance between schweschders is the worst kind of distance.*

*Take care.*

*Love,*
*Ruby*

A frown creased Mary's brow as she read the letter again. Although she knew that Ruby was simply trying to remind her of a time when they were inseparable, she couldn't help but feel as if the reminder was simply regarding Mary having ruined it all. She crumpled up the letter and tossed it in the waste bin before going in search of Caleb.

She found him in the shed bent over a table he was currently sanding. "I think you should take the job."

Caleb glanced up, confused for a moment before his eyes cleared. "But it's two counties away?"

Three weeks ago Caleb had received a generous offer from an Amish carpenter to take over his workshop. There were constant orders, repeat clients and the contracts he had for lumber came in much more affordable than the lumber Caleb currently had access to.

The only reason they didn't consider it was because it would mean leaving Caleb's and Mary's parents. But now, after the letter from Ruby, Mary knew she wouldn't be able to put the past behind her unless she was given a fresh start away from everyone and everything that reminded her of the vile thing she had done.

Moving would be her fresh start. "*Jah*, I think we should do it. A fresh start with our new *boppli*. Don't you think so?"

Caleb scratched his head and a smile lit up his face. "It's a *gut* offer, Mary. You'd never have to work again. We'll be financially secure, and the community…it's a nice one."

"How about the *haus*, did you ask where we were going to live?"

Caleb nodded, "The carpenter has a three-bedroomed cottage that comes with the job offer."

"Then it's settled," Mary said feeling the heaviness fall from her shoulders for the first time in years. "We can start over in a new community."

Caleb gave her a big goofy smile. "This is the best news ever. I know my parents would understand, but I thought you wanted to stay close to yours."

"We'll still see each other frequently," Mary promised although in her heart she knew this fresh start would mean cutting ties. She wouldn't send Ruby her new postal address and she'd see her parents once a month when it suited her.

No more brutal reminders of the past. No more feelings of inadequacy. No more wondering what happened to Jacob and if she had ruined his life as well. From now on it was going to be different. She was going to finally put the past and her actions behind her and focus on making sure her little girl had the best mother in the world.

"If you're sure, I'll send word in the morning," Caleb said.

"I'm sure, Caleb. We need this, I need this. Besides, I think it would be *gut* for Ella to grow up with her own memories instead of trying to recreate our childhoods."

Mary headed back into the house to check on Ella who was already in bed. Although the evening was cool the brisk breeze made Mary feel as if finally the cobwebs of her past could be blown away. She knew in her heart that this was akin to running, but it was time she moved on and if running was the only answer, then so be it.

## Chapter Twenty-Nine

For days Ruby waited for Mary's reply, but once again it didn't come. She tried to push it aside and go on with her chores as wife and mother, but every now and then she couldn't help but wonder if her sister hadn't received the letter or if she merely didn't want to write to Ruby.

At the bakery early on Saturday morning the answer came by way of a call from her mother.

"*Mamm?* Is something wrong? You hardly ever call us," Ruby asked as soon as her mother's voice came onto the line.

"*Nee, nee.*" Her mother sighed heavily. "I just miss you something terrible and wanted to hear your voice. How is my grandson doing? I can't believe he's eighteen months already." Her mother sounded tired and sad. Her mother didn't have to say the words hanging between them like the elephant in the room. Her son was eighteen months old and her mother had only seen him twice.

"He's growing something fierce. Every time I sew him a new piece, it barely lasts a month. How is *Daed*?"

"He's *gut*, although this thing with Mary is taking

its toll." Her mother's voice sounded wrong, as if
something terrible had happened.

Ruby's heart clenched remembering what her sister
was capable of but she quickly pushed it away. Mary
was a mother now, surely she had put the past behind
her as well.

"What thing with Mary?" Ruby asked, confused, as
Daniel glanced at her over his shoulder. "Is she alright?"

"Ach, you know how it's been. She's been withdrawn
for quite some time now. Barely ever talks to us or vis-
its, and just last week she and Caleb came by to tell us
they're moving."

"Moving?" Ruby repeated the word. For an Amish
couple to move was very unusual. Moving usually only
happened because of marriage, not after marriage. "But
why?"

"Caleb accepted a *gut* offer from a carpenter. Now
they're taking that darling little girl and moving two
counties away." Anna sniffed on the other side of the
line.

"*Mamm*, I'm so sorry to hear that." Without Mary's
family close by, her parents were all alone in the
community in which Ruby had been raised. Ruby
couldn't imagine how hard it must be for her parents.
First Ruby had moved away and now they were losing
their other daughter as well. Her parents had always had
a very tight knit family and she couldn't imagine her
mother surviving without her daughters living close by.

"*Jah, Daed* is taking it harder than I am. We always
dreamed we'd raise two beautiful girls and watch them
raise their *kinners*, but now... Ach, listen to me cater-
wauling like a five-year-old. I didn't phone to complain

or to make you feel guilty for finding happiness in Ohio; I just missed you something fierce."

"I know, *Mamm*. I miss you too. Just the other day Daniel mentioned I should come and visit, but if Mary's moving…"

"You should *kumm*," her mother said, elated at the news. "Oh, just wait until I tell your *daed*. He'll be so excited. But what about the bakery?"

Ruby smiled over at Daniel, "The bakery will be just fine. I'm sure the community can survive without my cakes for a few weeks. Daniel will be staying to take care of it."

"Will you be travelling alone with David? Oh, I don't know, Ruby, that sounds awfully dangerous."

Ruby laughed, "*Mamm*, a long time ago I travelled all the way to Ohio by myself, if you remember correctly. Am I mistaken or are you more protective of your grandson than you are of me?"

"Ach, don't mind me, I'm just a fussy pants. When will you be coming?" Anna asked as her voice grew excited. Ruby couldn't help but smile. Clearly her idea of visiting was exactly what her mother needed right now.

Ruby hadn't given the thought of visiting much more thought after Daniel had mentioned it and now suddenly faced with the commitment by hearing the excitement in her mother's voice, she knew she couldn't go back on her word. "Next month, perhaps. I'd need to cook in advance for Daniel, deal with a few things around the home, make sure I have clothes that will fit David."

Ruby laughed when her mother squealed, "Don't! Please let me sew him some when you get here. We can bake cakes and go for walks. You've just made my day, Ruby dear."

Ruby smiled, "I look forward to it, *Mamm*. Tell *Daed,* and if you see Mary, send her my love."

"Why don't you write her, Ruby?" the concern in her mother's voice made Ruby frown.

"What?" Ruby asked confused. "You didn't know?" Ruby took a deep breath not wanting to upset her mother but needing to make the truth clear. "*Mamm*, I have been writing Mary for years. The first time I received a reply was when Ella was born. It's like she doesn't want to write me." Ruby let out a heavy sigh. "I've put the past behind me, ever since I married Daniel, but it's as if she's refusing to let me be part of her life."

"That's very concerning. I thought things between the two of you had been fixed?" Anna asked, surprised.

"*Mamm*, I thought so too." Ruby sighed heavily. "I can't force her to write me. She's acting like I'm the one who betrayed her." She knew it sounded like sour grapes, but the way Mary was acting did hurt her, although she tried to ignore it.

"Keep the venom from your heart, my dear. Grudges only eat at happiness and you don't want a grudge to eat the happiness that little boy brings into your life."

"I know, I know…maybe when I come to visit, we can go see her. Maybe then…"

"*Jah*, you're right; maybe when you two have a chance to visit, things will look up." Anna sighed. "I honestly thought this was over. I can't imagine my two girls being at odds with each other, especially during such a special time in your lives."

They were both silent for a short while, both lost in their own thoughts about Mary and her obvious distancing from the family before Ruby finally spoke. "I'm glad you called, *Mamm*."

"Me too, but I best get going before everyone sees I'm holding up the phone shanty."

Ruby chuckled knowing that was the least of her mother's worries. No one ever used the phone shanty unless it was an emergency.

"I love you, *Mamm*, and I'll write to let you know when you can expect me and David."

"*Gut, gut.* I can't wait to tell your *daed*. I love you, Ruby, and send my love to Daniel and give that little boy a smacking kiss from his *grossmammi*."

The call ended and Ruby stood lost in thought for a moment until Daniel brushed a hand over her back. "Trouble back home?"

"*Nee*, at least I don't think so. Mary is moving away."

"Moving?" Daniel said in the same surprised tone Ruby had used when she heard the news.

"*Jah*, moving. My *mamm*… I told her I'd bring David to visit."

"That's a great idea. Didn't I once tell you all my ideas are great?" Daniel asked with a cocked brow and a charming grin.

Ruby smiled, playfully swatting him with a napkin when a customer stepped inside.

"Back to work, Mrs. Fischer, your name isn't on the door for no reason," he teased as he turned and headed back into the kitchen.

Ruby glanced after him and her heart simply swelled in her chest. Often she wondered if she shouldn't thank Mary for her betrayal so long ago, because if Mary hadn't intervened in her engagement with Jacob she would have never fallen in love with the handsome baker she now called her husband.

Ruby turned to a customer who had just entered the bakery with a smile. "Welcome to Ruby's."

"Are you Ruby?" the man asked curiously.

Ruby nodded. "I am. How can I help you today?"

"I've heard good things about your cakes. My *dochder* is turning one soon and I'd like to place an order."

Although Ruby heard every word he said she couldn't help but think of Mary's *dochder,* Ella. Would she ever have the opportunity of baking a cake for Ella's birthday? Her heart clenched in her chest. There was so much she wanted to share with Mary but she didn't know how to penetrate the wall her sister seemed to have built around herself. She pushed the thoughts of Mary aside and decided to start planning today. The sooner she got to Lancaster County the better.

"Perfect. Tell me more about the cake you have in mind?" Ruby asked with pen poised over a notebook.

## Chapter Thirty

The new community and new home were exactly what Mary needed. To raise her daughter in a community without the constant reminders of her failures as a sister gave Mary the opportunity to focus on Ella instead of the past.

The three bedroom house was larger than their small two bedroom. The living area was spacious and the kitchen was a dream to cook in. The only thing in her entire new life that made her think of Ruby was the oven. No one baked a cake like Ruby. Ella was blossoming with the attention she got from the neighbors and the ladies in the sewing group.

As for Mary, she had finally found the happiness she had always dreamed of. Things couldn't be better for her and Caleb. The job was just as promising as he had hoped and the wages were more than fair. Mary didn't have to think twice when she wanted to buy a piece of fabric to sew a new onesie for her little girl.

She hadn't told Caleb that she hadn't given her sister her forwarding address. That piece of information she kept to herself. Ruby would find out she had moved, of that she was sure. Anna King wouldn't keep a secret like that from her daughter, but at least now she no longer feared her mailbox.

Mary didn't even think about Jacob that often anymore. In her own way she was beginning to make peace with the past, although she missed her sister terribly.

After Ruby's last letter, Mary couldn't help but remember how they had been inseparable as children. The lazy afternoons in summer, hot chocolate in front of the wood stove during winter, these were all memories Mary would cherish because she didn't think they would make more in the future.

How could she ever see her sister again without remembering the pain she had caused?

Her new home was a short walk from town and today Mary planned to spend the day exploring the surrounds. She had put Ella in a dress and precious little prayer *kapp* before she set her in the stroller Caleb insisted they buy. Although Mary preferred holding her daughter against her chest, she understood the need for a stroller, as even a baby could become heavy after a while.

Just as she was about to head out she noticed the next door neighbor walk over. Mary had seen her from a distance a few times since her arrival but she hadn't met her yet.

"Hullo!" the woman called out. She looked a little older than Mary but her smile was warm as she crossed the lawn. "I'm Lisa Lapp, please don't make any jokes," she laughed self-consciously as she looked into the stroller. "And who's this little girl?"

"That's Ella and I'm Mary. Mary Zook," Mary said with a smile.

Lisa stood up and held out her hand. "Welcome to

the community, Mary. It's nice to have a young couple as neighbors. The people who used to live here were nearing a hundred, probably not that bad, but they used to complain about the boys making a noise. I have two."

Mary smiled. One day she dreamed of having a little boy who took after Caleb, but for now she was more than content with Ella. "They sound like a handful."

"Ach, they are, but such a joy as well. Where are you two off to?"

"We're going to explore town and get a few things from the grocer." Remembering that fresh leaf, Mary added, "Can we bring you something?"

"*Nee*, I don't need anything. But I do think we should have tea later. What about when you come back, you come over and visit for a while?" The offer of friendship was so unexpected that Mary couldn't stop the smile from spreading on her face.

"That sounds *wunderbaar*."

After talking a little more about the community and a local curio shop, Lisa insisted Mary visit, and Mary and Ella headed off to town. As she walked she couldn't help but enjoy the fresh air. Everywhere she walked in her old community she had been reminded of her childhood with Ruby and Jacob, but here she only saw the possibility of making new memories.

They peeked into the curio shop, surprised to find everything from decorative teaspoons right down to hand carved toys, and then they headed to the grocer. Here, Mary realized coming to a grocer was a bit challenging with a stroller when she had to push a basket-trolley as well.

She carefully navigated the aisles only taking the absolute necessities since she needed to carry them home.

By the time she reached the check out point she was already not looking forward to the walk home.

In front of her the man paying for his purchases seemed somehow familiar. It wasn't until he was done that he turned around and Mary gasped with surprise.

"Jacob?"

A frown creased his brow before a smile lifted the corners of his mouth. "Mary King? What are you doing here?"

Mary shrugged, completely caught off guard. After he fled from their community because of her actions, Mary never expected to see him again. "I…uh… I live here now. My husband has taken a position as a carpenter in town."

Mary was babbling but she couldn't help it.

"Welcome. It's a nice community," Jacob said shaking his head. Mary waited for him to bring up the horrid past, but he glanced at Ella instead. "Your *dochder* is the spitting image of you, at least what I can remember. You look happy, Mary."

Although Mary had believed she was happy, it was Jacob's affirmation that brought a smile to her face. "I am happy, Jacob. I… How have you been?"

She swallowed past the guilt, not wanting to let it sour their meeting, but Jacob blushed before he answered her with a smile. "Married. I met a kind woman who did me the honor of becoming my wife. We're expecting our first. It's so *gut* to see you. When I moved here I couldn't believe how much I missed everyone." Jacob hesitated for a moment before he continued. "How's Ruby?"

Mary thought of all the letters she hadn't replied to before she answered. "She's well. She has a little boy they named after my *daed*. Her husband named the bakery after her."

Jacob chuckled. "She could always bake. Well, I'm sure you're in a hurry to get that one home. It sure was *gut* to see you. You take care of yourself and send my love to your *familye*."

Mary smiled although it didn't reach her eyes. She had moved to forget all the harm she had done and yet she had found Jacob right here in her new town. She paid for her purchases and started home, but the entire way she couldn't seem to imagine how Jacob could have been so kind to her.

After what she had done, she expected him to chasten her, to carry anger in his heart towards her and yet he'd been nothing but kind.

By the time she arrived home she couldn't help but feel guilty all over again. She had ruined something special for Jacob and Ruby and although they had both moved on, she couldn't seem to forgive herself. If someone had done something like that to her, she would never have been able to find forgiveness in her heart.

After unpacking her purchases, she put Ella down for a nap knowing she wouldn't go over to Lisa's just yet. First she needed to deal with the demons that had resurfaced from her past. Once they were safely tucked away into the corners of her mind, she would focus on building new friendships instead of mulling over the friendship she had ruined with Jacob.

# Chapter Thirty-One

It was Saturday morning and just yesterday a lady from the sewing group had suggested Mary take her quilts to the farmer's market. The lady who owned the stall there was more than happy to snap up beautiful quilts at a fair price.

Mary couldn't help but be slightly nervous as she carefully packed her quilts into the basket. She took a large one, big enough for a double bed and two smaller ones. She wasn't sure the lady would be the least bit interested, but she felt like it was time she took a chance.

After their brief meeting a few weeks before, she and Lisa had become good friends. Lisa was such a kind person, and Mary had quickly felt comfortable with her. Whenever they discussed children and motherhood Mary couldn't help but wish that she could share the same bond with Ruby. What were Ruby's thoughts on discipline and routine? At least twice a week they would set their chores aside and spend the afternoon drinking tea and discussing motherhood. It was something Mary had hoped she would share with Ruby, but she still couldn't gather the courage to write to her sister again.

She hadn't told Lisa of the trouble between her and Ruby, but often Lisa reminded her so much of Ruby.

Lisa was also in the sewing group and had eagerly encouraged Mary to go to the farmer's market today. It was quite a distance away and Lisa insisted on watching Ella while Mary and Caleb went to the farmer's market. So once the buggy was packed, Mary headed over to Lisa with Ella in her arms and a nappy bag by her side.

"Are you sure you're up to this? She'll nap in an hour, but until then she's going to demand your attention."

Lisa glanced over her shoulder at her sons fighting in the living room. At the ages of eight and ten they were both already starting to show their independent personalities. "Please let me have her. At least they can't bother me when I'm watching a *boppli*," Lisa laughed, scooping Ella up.

For a moment Mary wished her parents were closer. How her mother would have enjoyed watching over Ella for the day. She pushed the thoughts aside and smiled at Lisa.

Mary shrugged with a laugh. "If you're sure. I promise we won't be long."

Lisa shook her head, "Have you had any time to yourself since Ella was born? Go and enjoy the day. I've raised two sons, although they don't look like they amount to much at this moment." A chuckle escaped her. "The farmer's market is filled with interesting things. Go spend some time with your husband; I'm sure he'll appreciate it. We'll be right here when you get back."

Ever since Ella's birth, Mary had never left her in anyone else's care. The thought was both freeing and terrifying. But to spend the day with Caleb after nights of restless sleep and days of hard work with the move might be just what they needed.

Once Ella was settled in with Lisa, Mary walked back home with a skip in her step. Somewhere between Lisa opening the door and telling Mary to enjoy her day with Caleb, Mary had made the decision to write to Ruby again. This time it wouldn't be a formal letter like the one she had written after Ella's birth. This time it would be a letter sharing her life and hopefully mending the fences she had all but torn down between them.

When she arrived home the buggy was already hitched, the quilts loaded in the back and her husband was rubbing the horse's flank. Mary's heart swelled in her chest. She loved Caleb more than she had ever loved before. The worst part was knowing that she had ruined things for Jacob and Ruby when she had simply had a crush on Jacob. Her feelings for Jacob had never even closely resembled the love she felt for Caleb.

Caleb checked the time on his pocket watch. "It's about an hour's ride to the market, so we ought to be back before lunch."

Mary laughed, "Or we could just have lunch at the farmer's market." She stepped closer and smiled up at her husband. "Lisa insisted we make a day of it. It will be the first time we will spend time together since Ella was born."

Caleb's brows shot up, "You mean she'll take care of her the whole day?" He let out a low whistle. "She's a brave woman."

Mary chuckled. "Exactly. We'd better go before she changes her mind."

"Have you got everything you need?" Caleb asked, moving to help Mary into the buggy.

"*Jah*, so what are we waiting for? Take me for a buggy ride, Mr. Zook."

Caleb laughed freely as he walked around the buggy and jumped on. "You haven't said that to me since we courted."

It was a long ride and by the time they arrived at the farmer's market Mary was eager to stretch her legs. She had never seen such a large farmer's market in her entire life. There were rows and rows of stalls selling everything from preserves to wooden toys. The scent of freshly baked bread and fresh fruit hung in the air as she and Caleb began meandering through.

The quilt stall was just two rows down and when it came into sight Mary clutched the basket tighter at her side. "Caleb, I'm not sure about this. Surely she has the best quilters in the county quilting for her."

Caleb smiled, "You are the best quilter in the county now, so you'd best put on your best smile and pluck out that quilt."

Mary couldn't help but feel nervous as she approached the stall. The lady, a woman in her early fifties, had a generous smile but a narrowed look from years of needle point.

"Hullo," Mary began but her voice faltered.

Beside her Caleb took her hand and squeezed it for encouragement.

"Would you like to buy a quilt, dear?" the lady asked with a cocked brow.

Mary shook her head and took a deep breath. "I was wondering if you'd be interested in buying my quilts." There, she had said it, Mary thought with a relieved sigh. The worst the lady could do was say no.

She glanced at the quilts in the basket and frowned. "You been quilting long, child?"

Mary nodded. "Ever since I could remember. My *grossmammi* taught me and then my *mamm*."

"Hmmm. Let me see. You know I only stock the best quilts." She reached for one of Mary's quilts and inspected it before turning to Mary with a cocked brow. "Do you have more?"

Mary nodded as she took out the other two. Her heart was racing in her chest as if her entire life depended on this. It was the first time she sought an opinion on her quilting and she feared she would fall short of the lady's high expectations.

It felt like hours ticked by as the lady touched each quilt and examined the stitches and the composition of coloring. She hmm'd and aah'd quietly before she finally turned to Mary with a frown.

Mary's heart began to plummet into her shoes when she finally spoke.

"How fast can you make these?" she asked eagerly.

Mary tugged her bottom lip between her teeth nervously. "That one took me a week, but the bigger ones take longer," she pointed at the smaller quilt.

"I'll buy as many as you can make as often as you can make them." The lady named a price that nearly made Mary stumble backwards.

"That's an awful lot of money," Mary countered.

"This is an awful lot of work. I'm not going to sell your work if I don't think you're getting what you deserve. They've paid more for work far inferior to this."

"I have a baby girl," Mary said, wondering when she would have the time to quilt.

"Then you quilt when you can, and if you don't, you

don't. *Familye* always comes first. But when you do have a quilt to sell, you can bring it to me any time."

Riding high on the success of selling her first quilt, Mary pushed the advice aside about family coming first. She remembered Ruby's last letter and decided then and there that she wouldn't let another day go by without writing to Ruby. It was as if everything was signaling to her today. First Lisa and now a perfect stranger. The time for avoiding her family was over. She wanted Ella to have a full life and she wanted her to know her family. Perhaps if Mary was lucky she could get to know Ruby again as well and just perhaps things between them could again be like Ruby had mentioned in the letters.

If she was starting fresh she should give her sister the liberty of a fresh start as well. It was time the past was buried for good and they put their family first again. Caleb took her hand as they walked away from the stall and squeezed it tightly. "I'm so proud of you. I know your *familye* will be too."

She smiled up at him, grateful that he was always the rock of support she needed. "I know they will. I'm going to write Ruby as soon as I get home. Would you mind if I invite her for a visit?"

Caleb laughed, "I should have brought you to sell your quilts sooner. That's a *wunderbaar* idea, and while you're at it, you should invite your parents as well. In the month we've been here, Ella has already grown a few inches, I'm sure they'd love to see her again."

"That's another great idea. Now where shall we wander first?" Mary asked feeling content as she looked out over the variety of stalls in the market place.

"The food aisle, definitely," Caleb laughed. "Do you think they'll have chicken pie?"

Mary laughed, "I think they'll have every pie you can imagine and more. Ach Caleb, I'm so happy. I never thought my quilts would fetch such a *gut* price."

"I know, I'm so proud of you. Just promise me one thing; you won't let the money blind you into working yourself into a bend."

Mary shook her head. "Ella will always come first."

"But today, just for today," Caleb said with a mischievous smile, "we come first."

Mary nodded before glancing up at the sky. She felt the rays warm her face and thanked God for every breath she had taken up until that moment. Because for the first time in years, she knew everything would be alright. For the first time in years, she believed that there was a way through the muddy waters of her relationship with her family.

She had made a mistake and they had been ready to forgive her; finally it was time for Mary to consider forgiving herself as well.

As they walked, she and Caleb talked. They caught each other up on small things that they hadn't had the time to discuss and soon Mary found herself telling Caleb about running into Jacob.

"He looks happy. I was so afraid I may have ruined his life," Mary admitted quietly. Caleb was the only person to whom she could reveal her guilt over what had happened.

Caleb shrugged. "Happiness is something we find for ourselves. Perhaps you did him and Ruby a favor, seeing as he's married and Ruby's found happiness with Daniel."

The idea was so unexpected that Mary frowned. "Really?"

"*Jah*. Everything happens for a reason and although you acted out of jealousy, maybe even your actions were for a reason. It's time to put the past behind you, and it's time we talked of our future."

Mary chuckled. "Really, and what do you want to talk about?"

"I was thinking that Ella seems very lonely." Caleb cocked a brow and Mary couldn't help but laugh.

"Can she celebrate her first birthday at least before we start thinking of having more *kinners*?"

Caleb shrugged. "Well, with your quilts selling now, we can afford to have plenty more. How do you feel about five?"

Mary laughed, knowing he was only teasing her. She couldn't remember the last time they had such a carefree day. For a moment she felt guilty for having this much fun without Ella but then she remembered something her mother had told her on her wedding day.

*Mary dear, remember to always cherish your marriage. A marriage can be seen as the wheels on a buggy and if the wheels break, there is no moving your family lye forward.*

At the time she didn't really understand but now she understood perfectly. Although her little girl needed her, her husband needed her as well. For them to build a family with a future, they needed a little time to themselves just to reconnect and remember why they fell in love in the first place.

Mary glanced at Caleb with a broad grin. "Maybe even six, who knows we might get lucky and have twins."

Caleb chuckled. "We'll name them Sage and Thyme."

"Herbs! You want to name our *kinners* after herbs?" Mary asked exasperated.

Caleb nodded. "*Jah*, we can start a whole herb garden with Ella as the leader."

As he teased her, Mary turned her face up to the sun with a skip in her step knowing that she'd always cherish the time Lisa had allowed her to have with Caleb today. She made a mental note to offer to watch the boys soon so Lisa and her husband could have the same.

## Chapter Thirty-Two

Over the last week Ruby had done everything possible to ensure that Daniel would be alright while she went to visit her parents. The house had been spring cleaned, she had cooked all the meals in advance and all that was left now was to start packing.

Although she and David didn't need much, she couldn't help but check and double check everything as she packed. A smile curved her mouth on the Saturday afternoon as she went over the list she had made that morning. When it had just been her, she managed without whatever she had forgotten, but things changed when you had a little boy with a favorite blankie and toys he couldn't seem to live without.

Early the next morning Daniel would be taking them to the bus station to board for the long ride to Lancaster County. The last time she had made the trip had been for Mary's wedding, and now she wasn't even sure she would be seeing Mary during this trip.

She still couldn't believe her sister had moved away from the community in which they had been raised. Of course, Ruby understood that when opportunities came you took them, but with the distance Mary had put between herself and her family, it was just a little too coincidental. Was Mary trying to forget she had a family at all?

She pushed away the troubling thoughts when David came bundling into the house with the energy only a child could have.

"*Mamm, Daed* is back," he announced proudly. His sentences were still short but every time he used a new word Ruby's heart simply bloomed with pride.

"Are you excited for the trip tomorrow? We're going to visit *Grossmammi* and *Grossdaadi* in Lancaster County."

"Far away place," David said drawing his brows together in a frown. "David don't like far away."

"It's alright if you don't like far away, do you know why?" Ruby asked remembering how fussy he had been with their last journey to Lancaster County.

He shook his little head fervently and Ruby scooped him up. "Because at the end of it is a destination that will make it all worth it."

She blew a raspberry in his neck making him giggle with joy as Daniel stepped into the house. After kissing her briefly he glanced at the suitcases surrounding them. "Are you all packed?"

Ruby laughed, "Daniel, if only I knew. I packed everything I could think of and more, and yet it still feels as if I'm forgetting something very important. You know how David can get when he wants something specific."

"Did you pack his blankie and the wooden truck he's so fond of?"

"*Jah*, and the wooden train and the extra blankie,"

Ruby shook her head on a smile. "Honestly, I think I should unpack everything and just stay home. I can't stand the thought of leaving you here for a month…"

Ever since their wedding they hadn't been apart for more than a few hours and although Ruby knew that Daniel would be fine, she knew she was going to miss him every day.

"You're going to miss me?" Daniel acted surprised. "I'll be here when you get back. Besides, David needs this, your parents need this, and you need to find a way to get through to your *schweschder*."

A heavy sigh escaped Ruby, "You're right. It's tough being a grown up and having to make all these decisions yourself. Don't you sometimes wish we didn't have to?"

Daniel chuckled. "*Nee*, because then I couldn't have chosen to marry you. I wouldn't have our life any other way. Besides, absence makes the heart grow fonder. For all I know you'll love me even more when you get back."

Ruby chuckled shaking her head. "Sometimes, Daniel Fischer, you're simply impossible."

Daniel laughed, "That's why you love me. Why don't David and I go check on the horses and the chickens and let you finish in peace?"

"Really?" Ruby asked hopefully. She could get so much more done if she didn't have to stop every few seconds for juice or to listen to one of her son's babbling tales. "That would be *wunderbaar*."

Daniel smiled and scooped David up, tossing him playfully over his shoulder. "Let's go feed the chickens some, David."

David's abundant laughter sounded through the house as they walked out. As soon as the door closed behind them, Ruby took a deep breath and relished in the silence. She knew she would only enjoy the silence for a short while before she missed her men.

She set to work checking every suitcase twice and double checking the items off her list before she finally realized what was bugging her. She was travelling all this way and she wasn't even sure if Mary wanted to see her. She thought of Mary's little girl and wondered who Ella took after. Would she be as petite as her mother? Would her smile come from her father? The thought of playing with her sister's little girl brought another smile to her face until she remembered the coolness of Mary's last letter.

On a whim she grabbed the writing pad and a pen and sat down at the table. Perhaps if she wrote Mary before they made the trip to go see her, it would clear the air a little. There was so much to be said that had been left unsaid over the years.

Neither had ever spoken of what happened with Jacob. Perhaps it was time to bring it all out in the open, time to deal with it instead of just pushing it into the past.

*Dear Mary,*

*I hope this letter finds you well. I trust Gott's blessings have been with you during the move. I can only imagine how hard it must have been with little Ella at your side.*

*How I long to meet her.*

*Mary, I write this letter not in anger, with blame or for any reason other than love. I write this letter because the distance between us has become of great concern to me. I want you to know as you read this, that I have always loved you and that I always will. You are my schweschder and I hope we can become best friends once again.*

*I have given much thought to what happened between us and now with the clearer benefit of hindsight, I've come to realize quite a few things. We were both friends with Jacob, and I believe we both loved him as a bruder once. I apologize for not thinking of you when Mamm announced the arranged marriage. I apologize for not asking how you felt about it. I should have, I realize that now. I just accepted that you were happy with the arrangement and in concluding that, I unknowingly pushed you further and further away.*

*I know that you did what you did out of love for Jacob, not out of hatred for me. Although at the time it hurt more than I can possibly say, I have to admit that I've come to realize that I never loved Jacob the way I thought I did. Only when I found Daniel did I realize what true love is.*

*I forgive you, Mary. I forgive you for what you did and I hope that we can put this behind us. You were never solely to blame for what happened. We all were. If Jacob truly loved me, he would have come to me, he would have questioned what you said instead of just sending word that the engagement had ended.*

*I no longer want this to stand in the way of our relationship. I'd like to meet your little girl; I'd like to be a part of Ella's life just like I hope you can be a part of David's life. Mary, we have so much more to live for, to celebrate, to let the past come between us.*

*I forgive you and I have forgiven myself for
what happened. We have both found love, both
had kinners, and I think it's time we move on
with our lives and share our happiness like we
once used to. I hope this letter finds you well and
that when you see me you will once again be the
schweschder I once called my best friend.*

*David and I are coming to visit Mamm and
Daed for a few weeks. I hope that while I am there
we can journey to your new home. Congratulations on Caleb's appointment. Mamm tells me it
is a wonderful opportunity.*

*My dearest schweschder, I look forward to see-
ing you and to seeing our kinners play together.*

*I love you and hope that this letter didn't scrape
open old wounds; instead I hope it heals them.
Love, always.*

*Your schweschder,*
*Ruby*

Ruby brushed away the tear that had slipped over
her cheek as she slipped the letter into an envelope. It
had been hard to bring it all to the forefront, but hopefully that was what was needed for them to finally put
this behind them.

She placed the letter in her handbag to post the following morning before she boarded the bus. Just as
she turned to find David and Daniel, a sudden rush of
wind swept through the house. Although it was summer, the wind chilled her to the bone. She closed her
eyes, gasping at the sudden cool air, and suddenly her
heart clenched, and her mind filled with Mary.

It was such a strange feeling quickly replaced by sorrow. Even as Ruby's eyes drew together in confusion, she couldn't help but wonder where her sister was at that very moment.

## *Chapter Thirty-Three*

Mary and Caleb returned to the buggy in the late afternoon, hand in hand. It had been one of the best days of her life. Not only did she sell her first quilt, but she had spent the day with her husband. For the first time since Ella's birth, Mary remembered what it felt like to be a woman and not just a mother.

"Do you think Lisa will baby sit more often?" Caleb asked with a wink as he took the reins.

The farmer's market was equipped for the Amish folk and had water and feed available for the horses while their owners perused the numerous stalls.

Mary laughed shaking her head, "If Ella was on good behavior, I'm certain of it, however, if she wasn't…"

"Then we'll just have to bring her along next time," Caleb turned to the horse. "Step up."

It was a long journey home but Mary didn't mind. She had her husband by her side and money in her pocket for her quilt. It was a day well spent even though the chores might have fallen behind.

She couldn't wait to get home to write a letter to Ruby. The lady at the stall had been right, family comes first and for too long Mary had been brushing her family aside because of the guilt that wouldn't seem to go away.

It was time she forgave herself, Ruby thought as Caleb turned onto the asphalt road. The road was much busier than it had been that morning and she quickly picked up the horse's nerves whenever a car zoomed by.

The *Englischers* were clearly frustrated with the slow pace of the buggy and zoomed past them at every possible chance. Mary turned to Caleb to ask him a question, when suddenly the car trying to pass them slammed head on into another vehicle. It happened so fast that Mary barely had time to shield her face when the on-coming car hit their buggy. The last thing Mary saw before she was whipped into the air with the force of metal hitting wood was Caleb's eyes and the fear shining in them.

The next thing she knew she could feel a hard surface beneath her and noise surrounded her.

"Can you hear me? Hello, can you hear me?"

The voice sounded distant as if the person was talking under water. Mary felt a warm hand against her cheek, and she tried to force her eyes open. A blinding pain shot through her skull and she closed them again. She tried to nod but it hurt even worse when she moved.

"Don't move, honey, help is on the way. Just hang in there. I'm going to hold your hand, squeeze it if you can hear me."

Mary squeezed, barely, but the woman kept talking. As she lay on the asphalt with pain reverberating through every inch of her body, all she could think about was Caleb and the fear in his eyes. She tried to ask for him but her mouth wouldn't move, neither would her eyelids. It was if her body was saving all its energy to deal with the pain that rendered her speechless.

She heard the sirens approach and tried again to open her eyes. They were heavy as if she had been drugged but she managed to open them just a slit. She turned her head in the direction of the sirens and saw Caleb lying at the side of the road. Someone was sitting by the horse, stroking his neck as he lay in the grass, the buggy shattered beside him.

Mary tried to speak Caleb's name but all she managed was a groan. The pain was so bad. She closed her eyes again and let the fog cloud her brain, at least then it didn't hurt so much. The lady beside her kept talking, kept telling her to hang on but Mary barely managed to recall her own name.

Suddenly she was surrounded by men who talked fast and worked even faster. She felt them rolling up her sleeve and slipping a needle into her arm. One ran his hands over her legs and arms; she didn't have to ask to know he was searching for injuries.

"You're alright; we'll get you to a hospital. Just hang in there," the man said as Mary was lifted onto something. She felt the ground fall away beneath her as footsteps sounded around her. She forced her eyes open again just in time to see the ambulance she was carried into. She saw a figure lying on the side of the road and her heart clenched knowing it was Caleb. She would recognize him anywhere. She closed her eyes focusing on the words of the man by her side. "Just hang in there."

The words kept mulling over and over in her mind as the pain medication began to work. Family comes first.

She felt the wet warm tear slip from her eye as the

sirens sounded and the ambulance raced to hospital. During the length of the journey all she could think about was Ruby and her parents. For how long she had pushed them aside, tried to distance herself from them simply to spare her own conscience.

What she had done was wrong, but avoiding her family because of it had been worse. She remembered Ruby's letters; her mother's caring words and her father's reserved smile. She should have apologized sooner, she should have allowed them back into her life, but instead she had pushed them away.

Another tear followed the first as she admitted for the first time that she had always been jealous of Ruby. Ruby had always been the prettier one, the smarter one, the one people liked more. If she was honest, there wasn't a time she had not been jealous of Ruby, and the worst was knowing that Ruby was the better person.

Ruby had been ready to forgive her on the day of her wedding, but instead of accepting her sister's forgiveness, she had carried around the blame and the guilt for years, causing it to eat away at her happiness. Not once did she explicitly apologize to Ruby. Not once did she own up to what she did to Jacob and apologize to him. She heard the beeping of machines and wondered if it was now too late. Would she ever have a chance to say sorry, to make things right with her family? Her thoughts circled back to her little girl and another tear slipped over her cheek. Ella barely even knew her family because of Mary. What type of mother kept a child from her family?

And Caleb...

Caleb had always been so strong, so supportive; not once did he question Mary's reticence to contact her family. She thought of him lying at the side of the road, she couldn't even remember if she had noticed any injuries.

"I'm going to give you something for the pain now," a voice spoke above her.

She felt the cool liquid seep into her arm before her mind grew fuzzy. The darkness enveloped her with a gentle embrace that pushed away the pain in her head, clearing it for just a brief moment. Just long enough to pray for Caleb and Ella and for the chance to see her family again.

"She's out," the paramedic notified the other. "It looks like a concussion, a really bad one and there might be some internal bleeding as well."

The attending paramedic sighed in response, shaking his head. "Did you see the buggy, or rather the scraps of wood lying by the side of the road? I don't get why people have to insist on rushing everywhere. These poor people had no chance of getting out of the way before the wreckage slammed into them."

"Let's just hope we can save her." They shared a concerned look before checking the monitors again.

"We'll be at the hospital soon enough."

The ambulance raced through the streets, a woman's life was at stake. Although they didn't know her, they were going to try everything in their power to save her.

Enough lives had been lost for one day on the small back roads.

## Chapter Thirty-Four

Ruby was standing in the kitchen early the following morning, packing snacks for the road trip. She couldn't be happier to be leaving for Lancaster this morning. After that strange feeling had swept over her yesterday, she couldn't seem to stop thinking about Mary. David and Daniel were taking care of the morning chores before they left for the bus in two hours, when there was knocking at the door.

She wiped her hands on a kitchen towel before heading to the front door. No one visited on Sunday mornings, especially not church Sundays. She couldn't help but feel a sense of trepidation as she opened the door. That sense only intensified when she saw the bishop with his hat in his hand.

"Bishop?" Ruby asked feeling the hairs on the back of her neck rise.

"Good morning, Ruby. Is Daniel here?" the bishop glanced over her shoulder into the house just as David and Daniel approached from the barn.

"Good morning, Bishop," Daniel called out with a

smile, but it quickly faded when he saw the expression on the bishop's face.

"Good morning, Daniel. I was hoping to have a minute with you and Ruby."

Ruby glanced at her husband and the only thought that swept through her mind was for her sister. The feeling she had yesterday had to be a warning or a premonition of sorts. She cleared her throat and turned to David. "Honey, why don't you go and feed the ducks before you leave? Remember to say goodbye."

"Going somewhere?" the bishop asked when David rushed off to the small duck pond in the yard.

Ruby nodded but she didn't answer. "Is this about my *schweschder*?"

Daniel's confused expression didn't even register as the bishop slowly nodded. "*Jah*, I'm afraid it is. I think it's best if we sit down."

"Of course," Daniel led them to the rocking chairs on the porch and once they were all seated, he reached for Ruby's hand. "What's happened, Bishop? If it was *gut* news, I doubt you would have come to pay us a personal visit."

The bishop sighed heavily as he glanced at his hat in his lap. "I'm afraid it isn't *gut* news. Your *schweschder* and her husband were in an accident yesterday. Their bishop contacted your parents who in turn contacted me."

"An accident?" Ruby asked remembering the rush of wind and the feeling of concern. "Is Mary alright?"

The bishop glanced at Daniel before meeting Ruby's gaze. "They were travelling home after a day at a local farmer's market. On the way back, there was a head-on collision between two vehicles; the wreckage of one slammed into their buggy."

Ruby's hands flew to her mouth. "Ella?"

"I take it Ella is their little girl?" When Ruby nodded, the bishop continued. "The *boppli* was with a neighbor for the day so she is unharmed, but your *schweschder*…" The bishop took a deep breath and sighed heavily. "Your *schweschder* is in an *Englisch* hospital. Although she didn't suffer many injuries, she suffered a very bad concussion. She is yet to wake from it. Her husband, regardless of all efforts by paramedics and doctors, couldn't be revived. They believe his neck was broken when he was flung from the buggy."

Ruby heard a muffled cry, not even realizing it was her own as Daniel's arms folded around her. "My *schweschder*, my poor *schweschder*," she said as tears streamed over her face.

"She's in a coma, Ruby, the doctors aren't sure she'll recover from this. I think it's best you head to Lancaster at your soonest convenience."

Ruby glanced at the bags by the front door and laughed ruefully. "I was heading there today. I wanted to make peace with my *schweschder*, get to know her *familye*, but now…"

"Would you like me to give you a ride to the bus station?" the bishop asked, concerned.

"*Jah*, that would be *gut*," Daniel answered before Ruby could deny the offer.

"But Daniel, how would you get home?"

"I'm not coming home. My *familye* needs me. I'm not letting you face this on your own. If you give me ten minutes, I'll be ready to leave."

"But the bakery?" Ruby asked, shaking her head. "The animals…we can't just leave."

The bishop placed a hand over Ruby's and squeezed it tightly. "We'll take care of everything, Ruby, just like we know you would if the roles were reversed. I promise your animals will be taken care of and the bakery will be seen to. You won't lose business because of this. In times of need, we pull together, and this more than qualifies. I'm sure your customers will understand if the bakery doesn't stock your specialty cakes for a short while."

Ruby nodded, swallowing back the tears. She had to get David; she had to help Daniel pack, but more than anything she needed to know her sister would still be alive when they got to Lancaster County.

She thought of the letter in her purse and wondered if her sister would ever get the chance to read it. Had she waited too long?

She stood up and did the only thing she could think to do. She carried the bags to the bishop's buggy. All that was left now was to get to Lancaster County and pray she wasn't too late. She thought of Mary's little girl who had just lost a father, her parents who had just lost a son in law and hoped their daughter wouldn't be added to the list of persons lost on this wretched day.

## Chapter Thirty-Five

Whenever her mind seemed to push the fog aside, Mary tried to open her eyes, but every time it dragged her under before she managed to gather the strength.

She had no perception of time or place; she knew only that there were people around her and that they were talking in hushed tones. Their voices disappeared as she was dragged under again. It didn't seem to matter that she was tired of sleeping, her body refused to do anything else.

She felt a hand close over hers and she drifted off only to wake up again with voices at the side of her bed.

She heard a little boy's voice before it was drowned out by the buzzing of her mind, before sleep dragged her under again. It felt as if it was a never ending cycle of battling to wake up before her mind shut down and succumbed to the sleep.

"Mary, Mary, can you hear me?" the voice sounded familiar, the hand was warm in hers, but she couldn't seem to place the voice.

"Mary, it's me. *Mamm*. Come on, honey, open your eyes. Open your eyes for me," her mother's voice turned to pleading. The hammering behind her eyes wouldn't stop but Mary took a deep breath and gathered all her courage before she finally forced her eyes open. The light was bright, too bright. As if in realization, the lights were suddenly dimmed, making it easier for Mary to look around her.

She was covered in white sheets, the walls were white and there were machines standing around the bed. But that wasn't what caught her attention; it was the three faces smiling down at her. Her heart swelled with love as she looked into her mother's eyes. Her father quickly brushed away a tear as Ruby moved closer and took her hand. "There you are. I knew you would be too curious to sleep through another visit."

Mary tried to speak but her throat was dry, as if someone had used sandpaper to scrape away the moisture. Ruby held a glass of water to her mouth and she sipped gratefully.

"*Denke*," Mary cleared her throat a few times before she managed to speak. "What day is it?"

"It's Wednesday. You've been in and out since Saturday," her father answered firmly.

Mary's eyes widened as she remembered the accident. Caleb lying on the asphalt, the buggy shattered as paramedics rushed through the wreckage towards them. "Ella?"

"Ella is safe. She's staying with your neighbor until you're better. How do feel, honey?" her mother asked gently.

Mary tried to smile but failed. The headache was too bad, the lights already too bright. She closed her eyes and tried to form the words she needed to ask. "Where's Caleb?"

"Hush now. Just rest." This time it was Ruby who spoke.

Mary forced her eyes open and looked at her sister. After everything she had done, after the heartache she had caused through her betrayal, her sister was still standing at her bedside in her time of need. "You came?"

Ruby chuckled sadly, "Of course I came, *dummkopf.* You're my *schweschder.* Rest, we'll talk later."

Mary didn't have to be told twice. She closed her eyes and felt the welcoming numbness of sleep envelop her again.

When she woke again, it was dark outside. She tried to look around the room but it was too painful to move. Instead, she stared at the roof in the hopes that someone would realize she was awake.

A hand closed over hers and she looked sideways to see Ruby standing over her with love shining in her eyes. "Ruby, where's Ella?"

"Ella is with Lisa. *Mamm* and *Daed* went to see her. I stayed with you. How are you feeling?"

Mary shook her head. "Like I was in an accident. I need to see Caleb. Is he alright? He…"

Mary trailed off unable to relive what she had seen at the scene of the accident.

Ruby squeezed her sister's hand, "I'll get the doctor."

Mary closed her eyes but heard the doctor return with Ruby. She couldn't believe Ruby had come all this way. After the way she had treated her sister these last few years she wouldn't even have blamed her if she hadn't come. She thought of all the letters she never replied to and pushed the guilt away. Seeing Ruby now was a second chance. It was a second chance at life for both of them. She wouldn't let the past stand in the way of their relationship for one more second.

"Mary, can you hear me? This is Doctor Sampson."

Mary opened her eyes and saw the tall man standing beside her. In a way that doctors had, he took her hand but only for the purpose of checking her pulse. "How are you feeling?"

"Tired, and my head hurts."

The doctor smiled kindly, "You have a very bad concussion; it's bound to hurt. Anything else?"

"*Nee*. Where is Caleb?" Mary asked, looking him in the eye. She didn't have to wait for his answer to know what it would be. She turned away and felt the first tear slip over her cheek as he spoke.

"I'm sorry, Mary, Caleb didn't make it. The impact was too hard, too sudden. He never made it to hospital."

Mary didn't respond, she didn't even look at the doctor again. She could only think of that last moment that Caleb had smiled at her before the accident. His kind smile, his gentle eyes and the way he could always make her smile. She had taken such a long time to find a man she could love and now he had been ripped away from her.

She heard Ruby and the doctor talk, but she didn't register the words. Her heart ached with sorrow as tears streamed over her cheeks. Her body began to shake from the shock, but she didn't even realize; all she could think of was that her little girl was never going to know her father.

As the pain ricocheted from her heart to her head, Mary couldn't help but regret ever going to the farmer's market. If she hadn't had the idea of selling her quilts, if they had just stayed home, if they had left a little later, or a little sooner... As the what if's continued in her mind, she saw her sister move towards the bed.

She expected Ruby to tell her to be strong, to think of Ella, but her sister simply leaned over her and held her close while she cried for her husband. When the tears finally subsided, Ruby brushed the hair from her face like she had when they were little girls. "We'll get through this, Mary, together; we're going to get through this."

Mary nodded and swallowed past the grief that tasted like bile in her throat. *"Denke* for coming, *schweschder."*

Ruby's mouth tugged into a sad smile. "Would you believe me if I told you I was already on my way before I heard about the accident? I was coming to see you, coming to mend our relationship. I missed you so much."

Another tear slipped from Mary's gaze. "I missed you too. Ach Ruby, how will I go on without Caleb? He was my everything. He loved me, regardless..." she sniffed, and the tears consumed her again. This time Ruby held her hand until the tears stopped and the pain teased her back to sleep again. Mary didn't even fight against the sleep or the medicine she was getting through the IV. Hopefully, sleep would numb her aching heart. Hopefully, when she woke up it would have all been a bad dream, all of it except for Ruby coming to visit.

# Chapter Thirty-Six

Ruby walked out of the room to get some fresh air, needing to clear her mind before she joined Mary again.

"My poor *dochder*, to lose her *mann* at such a young age…" Anna King drifted off, clutching her husband's hand.

"What did the doctor say about Mary?"

Ruby turned to her father and wished she had better news. She swallowed back the tears knowing that she needed to be strong for her parents. Her parents who had already lost a son in law wouldn't be able to cope with the loss of their daughter as well. "The doctor said the concussion is pretty bad. Mary has swelling on her brain and the fact that she keeps falling asleep isn't a good sign."

"What does that mean?" her mother asked with a furrowed brow.

Ruby wished Daniel was there to give her the strength she so badly needed at that moment. But it had been a unilateral decision that it would be best for him to stay at Mary's house with David.

"It means the prognosis isn't good. We should spend

as much time with her as we can," Ruby said trying her best to be courageous, but it wasn't easy when you knew you were preparing to say goodbye.

"Isn't there something they can do?" her father asked, concerned.

"*Daed*, they're doing everything they possibly can. Sometimes the injuries are just too significant even for modern medicine…" Ruby trailed off as she reached for her sister's limp hand.

Her mother let out a muffled cry before her father pulled her into his arms. "There now, Anna, it's alright. She's always been stubborn; she won't let this get her down."

The sobs grew louder and Ruby wished there was something she could do. Her father looked at her over her mother's head and shook his own. "I'm going to take her outside."

"*Daed*, take her home. I'll stay with Mary." Ruby brushed away her own tears as her father nodded.

"I'll bring her back in the morning; I think it's best if she was with Ella and David now."

Her mother didn't even look up as they made decisions for her. For the first time in her life Ruby realized her parents were growing older. In this time of crisis it was as if they had placed her at the head of the family. A position Ruby had never sought.

"That's a *gut* idea. Send my love to David and Daniel."

When they had arrived in town, Daniel had headed straight to Mary and Caleb's home with David. He promised to check in on the neighbor taking care of Ella. Ruby wished she could be with her family right now, but she wouldn't leave her sister's side.

After her parents left, she stepped back into Mary's room. She sat by her bed and let the tears finally come. Her sister was fast asleep; the only sign of life was the machine beeping softly beside the bed. So many regrets washed over her. She should've come to visit sooner. She should've tried harder to reconnect with Mary. She should have...

The thought trailed off when Mary whimpered in her sleep. The doctor had used so many terms she didn't understand; the only words she remembered were that Mary didn't have very much time. They were doing everything to keep her comfortable but the bleeding on her brain wouldn't abate.

Ruby finally brushed away her tears and thought of baby Ella. A little girl she hadn't yet met but already loved as her own. Ella had just lost her father and unless a miracle happened, she would lose her mother as well. She took a deep breath and closed her eyes with her hands clasped around Mary's.

*Dear Gott, please stay with my schweschder. Please heal her from these horrid injuries and bring her back to us. Please bless that poor little girl who has just lost her father. Go with my parents and give them the strength they need in this challenging time. I know everything happens according to Your will, Gott, but I ask now that You be merciful. Please Gott, protect, heal and bless Mary to see her dochder raised. I beg this of You, Gott, I beg this. Amen.*

When the prayer was finished, a nurse stepped into the room. She gave Ruby a kind look before checking the machines around the bed. "She's fast asleep. You're welcome to go home; we'll take good care of her."

Ruby didn't doubt the nurse's words for a single moment, but she couldn't bear the thought of going home and leaving Mary alone in the hospital. She shook her head defiantly. "*Nee*, I'll stay. If she wakes up, she needs to know we love her, she needs to know we're here for her."

"I understand. Would you like me to bring you a blanket?"

Ruby almost laughed. Her sister was fighting for her life and the nurse was concerned that Ruby was cold. "I'm fine, *denke*."

Once they were alone again, Ruby reached for Mary's hand. The memories rushed over her from as far back as she could remember, and her hopes were that they would share more memories in the future.

## Chapter Thirty-Seven

Every time she managed to fight through the pain and the fog of the medicine, it became harder. Every time it took more of her strength to focus and when she finally reached that clarity, Caleb's death struck her just as hard as the first time the words were spoken.

Mary sobbed as she opened her eyes. She couldn't believe her Caleb was gone. He had been such a wonderful man. So loving, so caring and it had taken a split second to end his generous life.

"I'm here, Mary, I'm here."

She heard her mother's voice through the pounding in her skull and sighed contently as her mother's hand wrapped around her own. She had lost all concept of time and place, all that she could focus on when she managed to open her eyes was whoever was sitting beside her. Tonight it was her mother.

Ruby had spent the night before with her in hospital. Although her sister didn't say much, just the thought of her staying had soothed Mary. The doctors had only told her she had a concussion but Mary had heard about concussions before. They were supposed to get better, not worse. There was something they weren't telling her, but she didn't have to guess what it was.

She was dying.

She could feel herself fading every time she fell asleep. She could feel the strength seeping out of her body and beyond that, she could feel herself giving up. Although she tried to fight against the pain and the drugged fog she was constantly in, she knew she couldn't fight much longer.

Mary thought of her little girl with her blonde wisps of hair and her beautiful blue eyes and her heart simply clenched in her chest. What would happen to her sweet little girl? She knew her parents would take care of Ella without hesitation, but they weren't her.

Mary and Caleb had such beautiful dreams of what they would teach their daughter and now…she might not even remember her parents at all.

The thought was so devastating that Mary couldn't even fathom it to be true. She wanted to be angry at God for taking Caleb, she wanted to curse Him for slowly taking her as well, but she knew she needed to accept His call.

It just wasn't easy when you knew you were going to leave a little girl behind, orphaned.

Mary swallowed back the tears she didn't want her mother to see and rolled over in the bed.

"Mary, are you awake?" her mother asked quietly.

Mary didn't answer. While she was clear of mind she had decisions to make. She had to think of Ella's future.

She could feel the medicine taking its toll again as her mind grew fuzzy but she fought against it. It seeped through her body, making her limbs feel heavy, making her mind grow fluffy like cotton wool as she felt her mother's hand on her back.

Tears burned the back of her eyes, knowing that her family had come. She had avoided them for such a long time. Letting her own guilt and shame push them out of her life and yet they had come. Even Ruby, who she had hurt intentionally, had come when she needed her.

She didn't deserve them, Mary thought as darkness began to envelop her. She didn't deserve their unconditional love and support but she was grateful for it. Because she had never needed them like she did now.

She forced her eyelids open; it took nearly all her strength to turn to her mother. "Caleb's funeral?"

The two words were those Mary had wished she would never have to speak, but she had to know when her husband would be put to rest. Her mother's eyes darkened with sorrow before a smile formed on her mouth. "We'll wait until you're better, that way you can attend as well."

"Ella?" The word slurred on her tongue. Mary blinked a few times to try and force the sleepiness away as the pain in her head dulled to a light throb.

"She's still with Lisa. We thought it best not to take her away from Lisa because she is familiar. I visit her every day." Her mother stroked her back, brushing her hair from her face as she summoned a smile. "Hush now, rest. You'll get better soon and visit with your little girl again."

The regret made her headache return with the force of a hammer blow. Why hadn't she taken Ella to see her parents more often? Now her little girl was staying with a neighbor because she knew the neighbor better than her own family. "I'm sorry, *Mamm*."

"There's nothing to be sorry about. You've always made me proud. You're a *wunderbaar mamm*, Mary; I can see it in Ella. She's a beautiful little girl, reminds me so much of you when you were that age."

Mary tried to smile but the pain was too overwhelming. "Ruby?"

"Ruby will be here in the morning. I told her to spend the night with David and Daniel. She'll be back at first light, I promise, she didn't even want to leave."

"I'm sorry, *Mamm*," Mary repeated the words. There so much she wanted to apologize for but she never had the time or the courage. She wanted to apologize for the pain she had caused her family with the Jacob fiasco, she wanted to apologize for moving away, for keeping Ella from them. But the strength wouldn't come, no matter how hard Mary tried to stay awake. She focused on her mother's eyes but her eyelids grew heavy and fluttered closed before she could say any of what she wanted to say.

She didn't hear her mother's answer as the light faded to black and sleep dragged her under. The last thing she thought of before she succumbed to the bliss of darkness was what would happen to her little girl if she didn't get better.

## Chapter Thirty-Eight

Five days after their arrival in Lancaster County, Mary's condition hadn't improved. If the doctor's words had frightened her on the day of their arrival, they now terrified Ruby. She could see Mary was slipping away slowly every day and it broke her heart because there was nothing she could do. The hollows in her cheeks were more pronounced, the dark circles beneath her eyes just another reminder how her sister was slowly losing her grip on life.

Twice her mother had asked her to meet Ella, and both times Ruby had refused. When she met Mary's daughter for the first time, she wanted Mary to be there.

She wanted to share the moment with her sister.

But sitting at the side of Mary's bed a little after midnight, she was beginning to realize that Mary wouldn't be there for that moment. She had been in and out of consciousness the whole day, every time enduring less than before.

Ruby prayed every second she had that her sister would recover to raise her little girl, but her hope was fading just as Mary's consciousness was.

Both her parents were taking it hard, only Daniel had been a pillar of strength since they arrived. He kept David busy, oblivious to his aunt's condition and made sure there were meals on the table whenever someone came home from hospital. He took David over to the neighbor's to play with his cousin every chance he got. Although it pained Ruby to know her husband and her son were spending time with Ella, she was exactly where she needed to be.

Ruby glanced out the window at the night sky and remembered the awkward feeling she had on Saturday. That moment when the wind had rushed through her house. She wasn't foolish enough to believe in premonitions but thinking back now the timing was in perfect sync to when Mary was in the accident.

Even miles away from her, Ruby had known something was wrong.

She took Mary's limp hand in her own and kissed it gently. "Come on, Mary, you need to fight. You need to come back to us." A tear slipped over Ruby's cheek when Mary's fingers squeezed her hand in response. She would never forget the antiseptic smell of the hospital. She would associate it with this dreadful time for the rest of her life.

"Don't cry, please don't cry," Mary's voice sounded ragged, as if she had smoked a whole pack of cigarettes recently. "*Mamm* cried enough this morning."

Ruby smiled through the tears and brushed them away. "We're just concerned. That's all."

Mary's eyes were open but they were heavy-lidded as if keeping them open was already taking more energy than she had left.

"I know that, but I can't stand the thought of you crying while I'm still here." A small smile lifted the corners of her mouth. Mary tried to adjust herself into a sitting position, but it clearly took a great deal of effort. "I've caused all of you enough tears already over the years."

"How are you feeling?" Ruby asked, concerned when her sister flinched.

"The light, if you switch it off, I'll feel better. The headache won't go away." She closed her hand over her eyes and waited for the light to be turned off.

Ruby got up and switched off the light. The headache was caused by the swelling on her brain that wouldn't subside. The doctors had warned them that the chances of an aneurysm were high if the swelling didn't soon abate. How soon was soon? Mary had been in and out for almost five days. She didn't seem to be getting any better; in fact it seemed she was only getting worse.

"That better?" Ruby asked taking a seat beside Mary's bed again.

"Much better. *Denke*." Mary sighed and tried to shift herself up in bed.

"Don't, Mary, you need to rest," Ruby tried to stop her.

"*Nee*, I need to talk to you," Mary insisted on a ragged breath as if the small movement had taken every ounce of her energy.

"We can talk tomorrow," Ruby assured her.

"*Nee*, I want to talk to you now," Mary insisted.

Ruby didn't want to fight so she'd listen but then she was going to call the nurse to give Mary something for the pain that paled her cheeks to the color of white linen.

"What is it, Mary?" Ruby asked gently, still clasping her sister's hand.

"I'm sorry, Ruby. I—I've never apologized for what I did to you and Jacob."

When Ruby tried to stop her, Mary shook her head. "Please, let me apologize. I was jealous. I know it was wrong, but I was so jealous. You had Jacob and I had no one. I just… I wanted him to see me and the only way that could happen was if he wasn't looking at you."

Mary stopped talking, trying to catch her breath. Ruby wanted to tell her it was alright but it was clear her sister wasn't finished yet. "Please forgive me, Ruby. I've distanced myself from my *familye* for too long because of this. The shame and the guilt wouldn't go away over what I did. I thought if I broke contact with you it would disappear, but it never did. Please forgive me, Ruby."

Ruby smiled and pressed a soft kiss to her sister's forehead. "I forgave you years ago, Mary. It's time you forgive yourself. We've never stopped loving you, we've always cared about you. It's time you forgive yourself. You made a mistake, we all make mistakes."

Mary sighed gratefully. *"Denke."* She leaned back against the pillows Ruby had positioned behind her head and smiled. "I know I don't have the right to ask any favors of you after what I did, but there is one…"

"Anything, Mary, just tell me what you need," Ruby assured, knowing her sister was going to drift away again soon.

"I'm dying, Ruby." The words weren't a question, they formed a statement. Hearing those three words from her sister's mouth hurt more than any words a doctor could have spoken.

*"Nee,* you're not. You're going to get through this," Ruby insisted as a tear slipped over her cheek. How

could she not cry when her sister was making these kinds of statements?

"I'm not a fool. I can feel myself growing weaker. The medicine doesn't help for the pain like it did a few days ago. I know it's happening, Ruby, I'm trying to deal with it, let me."

"There is still hope," Ruby mumbled, hoping she was right.

"You're right, there might still be hope; but if there isn't, I need to know Ella will be cared for." Mary took a deep breath and closed her eyes. Ruby could see the headache was taking its toll again. "I want you to take Ella. I'll sign whatever needs signing tomorrow, but I need to know that when I'm gone, you'll take Ella."

Of all the things Ruby expected her sister to ask, this was the last. She hadn't given it much thought, but she had subconsciously accepted that if something happened to Mary, her parents would take Ella. "If that's what you want, of course I'll take care of Ella."

"Like she was your own?" Mary asked forcing her eyes open. Her anguished gaze met Ruby's and she felt her heart break with sadness. How hard it must be for her sister.

Ruby took a deep breath and smiled at her sister. "After David…the doctors say I can't have any more *kinners*. I'll take care of Ella as if she were my own. I promise you, Mary."

Mary's eyes narrowed and a tear slipped over her cheek. "I didn't even know. I pushed you aside when I should've been there for you… We've lost so much time. My foolishness… I'm so sorry, Ruby."

Ruby forced a smile even though she wanted to cry

like there was no tomorrow. "We're making up for it now. Hush now, rest."

"Will they bring Ella to me tomorrow? I need to see her one last time."

"Of course. I'll make sure she comes tomorrow. Rest now, you want to be rested when she comes."

Mary didn't argue. She closed her eyes and through her breathing Ruby could tell she was in a lot of pain. Ruby quietly got up and went in search of a nurse. She found the nurses at the nurses' station and cleared her throat of emotion. "I need…my sister is in pain…"

The nurse met her gaze with empathy and stood up. "I'll give her something. Doctor said we should make sure she's comfortable. But it's hard to know when she's in pain because she's in and out the whole time."

Ruby nodded as she followed the nurse back to Mary's room. The nurse turned a dial on the IV and smiled over the bed at Ruby. Almost instantly, Mary sighed with relief.

The nurse left and Ruby held her sister's hand. Within minutes her breathing slowed to that of a deep sleep while Ruby sat at the side of the bed crying into her hands.

# Chapter Thirty-Nine

Ruby sat by Mary's bedside the entire night. When her mother came the next morning to relieve her, Ruby refused to leave. Last night had healed so many old wounds and her sister's request had shaken her to the core.

Mary wouldn't be asking this if she didn't know she wasn't going to make it. Her mother insisted again later that morning that Ruby should head home and take a bath and rest for a while, but Ruby didn't want to leave her sister.

"Ruby, David misses you. Go, spend some time with your *familye* and come back when you're rested."

Her mother had a point. She had barely seen David and Daniel since they arrived in Lancaster County and she did miss David terribly, especially after last night. Her father drove her home and as soon as she arrived she asked her father to send word to the neighbor that Mary wanted to see Ella.

"Ella's having a nap," her father announced when he returned to the house a short while later. "Lisa said she'd be down for another hour or so, then she'll let me drive them to the hospital."

Although she had just arrived, Ruby turned to Daniel, "I need to go with."

Daniel didn't argue, he simply smiled and nodded. "I understand. Go take a bath and spend some time with David, I'll call you when Lisa comes."

Ruby did as she was told. After a rejuvenating bath, she spent almost an hour playing with David and his wooden train. She tried to focus on her son but all she could think of was what Mary had said the night before. For years Mary had been carrying around the guilt, allowed it to eat at her until she had distanced herself from her family completely.

Ruby was grateful they had time to talk the night before, but she still couldn't imagine not having a sister anymore. She fought against the tears that threatened to fall when Daniel joined them. "How are you holding up?"

Ruby sighed and shook her head. "It's hard. I'm trying to be strong, but it's hard, Daniel."

"I can only imagine. I'm here for you. Whatever you need, you just tell me."

"Just take care of David," Ruby said with a smile, leaning into his waiting embrace. She remembered her sister's request and met Daniel's gaze. "Do you think David can stay with his *grossdaadi* while we go for a walk?"

Daniel frowned but nodded, "I'm sure your father would be more than elated."

Once David was settled with his *grossdaadi*, Ruby and Daniel headed outside. They walked around the house to the small field beyond before Ruby finally gathered the courage to say what she needed to say.

"Last night, Mary woke up for a short while. I insisted she sleep but she wanted to talk," Ruby started with a heavy heart. Their conversation had scraped over so many old wounds but the healing had already started as well.

"What about? Is she alright after finding out about Caleb?"

Ruby nodded. "She knows, although she's shattered. We spoke about the past, Daniel. We finally spoke about it and she's never forgiven herself. Last night I told her it was time to put it behind us. It wasn't just her fault; I should've known she loved Jacob…" A tear slipped over Ruby's cheek and Daniel slipped an arm around her shoulder.

"I can imagine it was hard. I'm glad you talked. You both needed it."

"She's fading, Daniel, I can feel it. It's as if she's weaker every time…"

"You heard what the doctor said." Daniel sighed heavily. "I wish there was something I could do to make this easier for everyone."

"You are, you're taking care of David, you're cooking, and you're here. That's already helped me just knowing you're close by. There's something else, Daniel…" Ruby trailed off.

"What is it?" Daniel asked rubbing her shoulder as if he were transferring strength from his heart to hers.

"Mary asked me if we would take Ella if…" she trailed off, clutching her hands to her throat. She couldn't imagine losing her sister.

"She wants us to be Ella's guardians?" Daniel asked gently.

Ruby nodded. "I hope it won't be necessary, Daniel, but she asked. I told her we would. I hope that's alright with you. I didn't even think to ask you first." Ruby realized she had made a lifelong commitment without even asking Daniel's opinion. "I'm sorry for laying this on you."

Daniel smiled and shook his head. "Of course it's alright. It's more than alright. We'd raise her like our own *dochder*. She's a beautiful little girl, Ruby, full of life and laughter."

Ruby nodded. "I'll meet her today." The words clogged her throat. It was hard to accept that the day she would meet her sister's daughter, would be the day she accepted the role as her mother. "I hope Mary makes it, Daniel. Last night…she apologized. For the first time, she really apologized."

Daniel nodded and drew her into his arms. "I used to believe that everything happens for a reason. What could be the reason for this, Ruby? What could be the reason for taking Caleb, and possibly Mary from their little girl? It just doesn't make sense."

When her husband's voice broke, Ruby felt the tears streaming over her cheeks. "We have so much to be grateful for. Here we were angry that we couldn't have more *kinners*, where Mary might never even see her *dochder* grow up."

"We'll be more grateful, Ruby. We'll thank *Gott* every day for our blessings and we'll stop asking for the things we don't need."

Ruby nodded when she heard a door close in the distance. "Lisa is probably on her way."

"*Kumm*, I'll walk you to the buggy."

As they rounded the house, David stood with his *grossdaadi* on the porch as the neighbor arrived with a beautiful baby girl in her arms.

At six months old Ella was the spitting image of Mary at that age. Ruby felt her heart swell with love and without a single word she reached for the baby girl. She expected Ella to cry because a stranger was taking her from familiar arms, but instead she smiled up at Ruby as if she knew she was her aunt. She smelt like baby, powder and milk. She was so innocent, unharmed by the ruthlessness of life. Ruby's heart clenched knowing that Mary wanted to say goodbye. Ruby held the baby close and she didn't even try to wriggle free, instead she buried her face in Ruby's neck and Ruby had to bite back the tears that threatened to fall.

Ruby smiled at Daniel over the baby's head and knew she would have no trouble at all raising this little girl as her own.

Now she only prayed that it wouldn't be necessary.

Mary needed to get through this. She needed to be there for her daughter, Ella needed her. Ruby sniffed knowing the truth she had tried to reveal in her letters for such a long time: she needed Mary as well.

They needed to make more memories together before she could walk through the pearly gates.

## Chapter Forty

~❧~

They arrived at the hospital shortly before five in the afternoon. Ella had remained on Ruby's lap for the duration of the trip to the hospital, to Lisa's astonishment. Ruby couldn't take her eyes off the beautiful little girl as she pointed out flowers and cows in the distance.

Walking into the hospital, Ruby handed Ella back to Lisa. She wanted a word with Mary first if she was awake.

Luckily Mary was sitting up in bed. Although she looked even paler than that morning, Ruby knew she was forcing herself to stay awake to see Ella.

"How are you feeling?" Ruby asked, approaching the bed.

"Like my head is about to explode, but I asked the nurses to hold back with the medicine. I don't want my mind fogged today, although it hurts."

Ruby nodded. "I wish things could have been different. I wish you didn't have go through this pain. Just tell me when I need to call them for more medicine."

Mary nodded. "Did you bring Ella?"

Ruby smiled although her heart was breaking in her chest. "You ready to see your little girl?"

Mary nodded. "I'm feeling like this can't be the last time." A tear slipped over her sister's cheek and Ruby felt one slip over her own.

Ruby reached for her sister's hand. "It won't, you'll get through this. I know you will. Everyone is praying for you."

Mary shook her head. "The doctor was here this morning…it's only going to get worse…the pain…" Mary sniffed and wiped her tears. "I don't want her to see me cry. Promise me you'll take care of her, Ruby?"

Ruby swallowed past the emotion in her throat. "We'll take *gut* care of her, I promise you. I met her on the way here, she's wonderful, Mary. She reminds me so much of you."

"Just promise me one thing," Mary urged weakly, reaching for Ruby's hand. "You'll tell her about us."

"Of course," Ruby promised as the door opened and Lisa walked in.

The moment felt too intimate to watch but Ruby couldn't make herself leave the room. Ella playfully gurgled and bubbled as Mary whispered to her. Tears slipped quietly over Ruby's face as she watched Mary and her daughter. She couldn't help but wonder if Mary would see her daughter again. The moment was so special, as if Mary was saying goodbye already.

When Mary's strength seemed to fail, she glanced up at Ruby with tears in her eyes. "Ruby?"

Ruby knew Mary couldn't hold Ella any more. Her strength was disappearing, the pain overwhelming her every breath. She took Ella from her mother's arms and it broke her heart. Would Mary ever hold her daughter again? She met Mary's gaze and tried to communicate how much she loved her.

Instead of leaving, she sat with Ella on her lap and pressed the call button for the nurse. Within seconds the nurse was in the room. She gasped when she glanced at the monitors. "She's in a lot of pain."

Ruby nodded. "I know. She wanted to say goodbye to her little girl."

Ella wailed in her lap but Ruby didn't leave. While the nurse gave Mary something for the pain, she sat by her side, holding her sister's hand with her one hand and her other wrapped around Mary's daughter. It wasn't long before Mary fell asleep.

"Could you ask the lady outside to fetch the baby?" Ruby said with a ragged voice. Lisa had agreed to wait outside the room if she was needed for Ella.

The nurse nodded and Ruby could see the fear in her gaze as well, Mary didn't have a lot of time left.

The door opened softly a few seconds later and Lisa stepped inside. Ruby stood up and handed her Ella. Lisa glanced at the bed and a tear slipped over her cheek even as her eyes widened with surprise.

Lisa excused herself from the room, clearly shocked at Mary's condition. Ever since the accident, Lisa had been taking care of Ella and hadn't seen Mary since the Saturday morning when Ella was dropped off.

Once Lisa had left, Anna returned to Ruby's side. Ruby knew how hard it was for her to see her sister fade, but she could see the last few days had wrecked her mother.

Her mother stepped towards her and rubbed a hand over Ruby's back. "She told me…"

Ruby nodded, not wanting to cry.

"It's the best thing for that little girl. You and Daniel will be great parents to her."

Ruby nodded, still unable to speak. "Go with Lisa, *Mamm*, take Ella home. She needs to be with *familye* now. Mary needs to rest."

Her mother sighed as she glanced at the bed where her other *dochder* was sleeping. She leaned over Mary. "I love you, *dochder*."

When she turned to Ruby this time her eyes were filled with tears. "I'll take care of Ella; you take care of Mary, just like you did when you were small."

The reference to their childhood made Ruby's heart clench in her chest. To know she would never have that time with her sister again. She nodded and smiled through the tears at her mother.

When her mother left the room, Ruby took Mary's hand and held on tighter than ever before. "I won't let you down, *schweschder*. I'll do everything in my power to make sure that little girl gets all the happiness she deserves. I love you."

She had barely finished speaking when one of the machines started sounding a flat monotonous beep. Ruby didn't have to be medically trained to know what it meant. She kept hold of Mary's hand even as doctors and nurses rushed into the room. Only when they asked her to step aside, did she relinquish her hold. Not a single tear flowed over her cheeks as she watched them trying to revive her sister.

It was the hardest moment in her life but in her heart she knew Mary was in a better place now. She was now in a world without pain, she was with Caleb and she walked with God. She couldn't help but be grateful that they had brought Ella to say goodbye just in time. She stood aside and watched the doctors step away from the bed one by one. One person called out the time, while another marked it down on a chart even as their happy childhood came in flashes to Ruby as she glanced at her sister's lifeless body on the bed.

The doctor turned to her with kindness in his eyes. "We tried everything we could…"

"I know." Ruby offered in return. "I think she just waited to say goodbye to her little girl."

"My sincerest condolences." The doctor touched her shoulder before leaving the room. One by one the nurses offered their condolences before the last one turned to Mary before she stopped by Ruby. "I'll give you some time to say goodbye."

Ruby nodded, wishing she didn't have to say good-bye. She had come to Lancaster County to reconnect with Mary and now she had to bury her. The thought pierced at her heart and made the tears burn her eyes like hot coals.

Alone with Mary, Ruby closed her eyes and let the tears come. She knew they wouldn't stop until she let them pour out of her with all the love and sadness that overwhelmed her.

She had prayed for a little girl for so many years, but not once did she imagine that she would lose her sister to have the prayers answered. For a brief moment she felt angry at God and the universe for making things happen this way, before she realized this was no one's fault.

It was an accident. An accident that ruined a family, but she could still make sure that Ella had a family. She would shower Ella with all the love that the little girl deserved and raise her as her own.

When the sobs finally subsided, she wiped her face and lifted her head to glance at her sister one more time. She touched her sister's already cold hand and closed her eyes. "I love you, Mary."

She stood like that for a moment, remembering all the good times and the good memories before she walked out. It was time to tell her family, and although Ruby wished it could be different, she knew the news would be better coming from her.

She walked out of the hospital and found her parents, Lisa and Ella standing beside the buggy.

"There you are. We were just about to leave..." her mother's words trailed off as her hands closed over her mouth.

Ruby swallowed and met her parents questioning gazes. "Her suffering is over. She walks with *Gott* and Caleb now."

She didn't wait for her mother's response, she didn't search her father's eyes for strength, instead Ruby walked over to the little girl in a stranger's arms and scooped her up.

Because now Ella was all she had left of her sister.

Ella smiled up at her and tugged on a piece of hair that had escaped from beneath her prayer *kapp*. A smile tugged at the corners of Ruby's mouth even though her heart was bleeding for the little girl in her arms. "You had the most wonderful *mamm* in the entire world," she whispered to Ella as she bit back the tears.

## Chapter Forty-One

Three days later, Ruby stood with Ella in her arms, David on her one side and Daniel on the other in front of the open graves. She still couldn't believe that both Mary and Caleb had been taken from them so suddenly. Her mother and father stood just on the other side of David, both devastated by the loss of their daughter.

They didn't postpone the funeral any longer than it took to hand dig the graves. It was time for Mary to rest, her mother had insisted.

No one mentioned the hard times Mary had brought on their family, or the way she had withdrawn herself from them in recent years. Instead, as if they had made a pact, they only spoke of the good memories.

When they arrived home from the hospital, Ruby had accompanied Lisa to fetch Ella's things before bringing Ella home with her. She would always be grateful to Lisa for taking care of Ella while Ruby and her family spent the precious time with her sister, but Ella was hers to take care of now.

Ruby knew that paperwork and red tape were necessary for her to become Ella's legal guardian, but she didn't care about that now. In her heart she knew everything would work out the way it was supposed to.

Ella would become part of their small family because that's the way Mary had wanted it.

Ruby still couldn't believe how fast everything had happened. What was meant to be a holiday to make up for lost time had become a devastating goodbye to her sister. Ever since taking Ella in her arms at the hospital, she had barely let the little girl out of her sight.

Her last promise to her sister was that she would take care of her daughter and it was a promise she would keep for the rest of her life. She would teach Ella how to sew and tell her about her mother's talent. She would teach her how to bake and tell her all about her mother's favorite chocolate cake.

When the doctor told Ruby that she would never be able to have another child, Ruby had been devastated. Now Mary had given her a child, a beautiful little girl, and she would always be grateful for that gift.

It was breathtaking how similar Ella and David were in appearance. Anyone not in the know would be forgiven for mistaking them as siblings. Although Ruby would raise Ella as her own daughter, she would make sure that Ella knew about her parents.

Daniel and Ruby hadn't yet discussed returning to Ohio, but Ruby knew they couldn't wait too long. Besides the bakery that couldn't remain in the care of the community indefinitely, it was imperative that Ella was settled into her new life as soon as possible. Just the night before, once the children had been settled, her parents had asked her about Ohio and the community they lived in.

Ruby didn't have to ask to know that they were considering moving to Ohio to be closer to their grand-children. She thought of Aunt Elizabeth and wondered if she would be open to her parents staying there for a short time until they decided what they wanted to do. Now more than ever she knew her parents weren't going to be alright on their own.

They had just lost their daughter; they could not af-ford to lose the grandchildren as well, to distance.

The letter she had written to Mary still lay in her bag, but it no longer bothered her. Because late that night in the hospital, she and Mary had made their peace. They had both apologized and forgiven, if only they could have done that sooner, Ruby wished.

Ruby adjusted Ella on her hip when she began to squirm in her arms. As if the baby knew that her par-ents had passed away, she had been fussier than usual this morning. First, she didn't want to feed, and then she had cried for almost twenty minutes while Ruby tried to dress her. Not even Daniel, who had become her second favorite person, could calm her down. If anyone tried to soothe her, she only fussed more whenever she was consoled, and she only seemed to be content when she was in Ruby's arms.

It was a warm spring morning and people had come from all over to pay their respects to Mary and Caleb. Although the funeral ceremony would be held in their new community, overseen by their bishop, the bishop of their childhood as well as numerous friends and family had travelled from her parents' community to say their final goodbyes. The wind tugged at Ruby's hair as the bishop began the sermon.

The words were a kind reminder of having to be grateful for what we have, to realize how blessed you are to be healthy and alive and to remember what a blessing children were. Ruby listened and held onto little Ella, knowing that today was going to be the hardest day of her life.

When the sermon was finally over, the men lowered the plain coffins into the ground. Caleb had worn his wedding clothes for his burial while Mary was dressed in the wedding dress she had sewn herself. Ruby knew she would never forget the peaceful look on her sister's face, no matter how long she lived on this earth. The congregation grew quiet as the coffins were slowly lowered into the hand dug graves.

There were no flowers or popular songs as reminders of all they had lost. No reminders were necessary, and the tombstones would be no more than simple wooden crosses. When the men finally stepped back from the graves, the bishop picked up a handful of dirt and turned to the congregation. "May salvation await them in heaven. Amen."

He sprinkled the dirt over the lowered coffins and indicated for the family that it was their turn. Ruby knew that flowers did not form a part of their funeral traditions, but just once she wished she could drop a white rose onto the coffin rather than the handful of dirt.

She walked away from the open graves, holding David's hand in hers while carrying little Ella, and she heard Daniel by her side.

"Would you like me to take her?" Daniel asked gently.

Ruby turned to her husband and shook her head. She needed Ella today just as much as Ella needed her. "*Nee*, we're fine."

Behind them condolences were offered to her parents, but Ruby didn't care. She didn't need to hear how well respected and loved Mary had been among the community members; she knew how much Mary had meant to her. Although she had barely known Caleb, she would forever be grateful to him for making her sister happy and for giving them Ella.

There would be a gathering of sorts for a meal after the funeral, but Ruby wasn't ready to face the congregation just yet. Instead she walked to the shadow of a large oak tree and sat down beneath it. David jumped at the chance to escape his mother's grasp before running into the meadow.

Daniel laughed, shaking his head. "They're so resilient. Do you think he even knows that we just buried his aunt?"

Ruby shook her head, "I doubt it. For him it's just another day, the only difference is there is now a *boppli* living with us. Did you hear what he calls her?"

"Baby Ella, it nearly broke my heart when I heard it the first time."

"It's the sweetest thing," Ruby sighed.

"Let me go after him, before he goes too far." Daniel walked in the direction of David, leaving Ruby and Ella alone.

It was almost time for her feed and her nap but before she put her down, Ruby had something she wanted to tell the little girl looking up at her with an expectant gaze.

"Did you know that your mother and I used to play in the meadows back home? We used to chase butterflies and lie in the grass, just looking up at the sky. We'd guess the shapes of the clouds and the whole time we'd be holding hands. That's the type of friend your mother was. We're going to miss her so much, Ella, but I promise I'll tell you about her any time you want to listen."

## Chapter Forty-Two

Ruby was so focused on telling Ella about Mary that she didn't even hear the man approach her. When a towering man suddenly spoke beside her, her heart skipped a beat.

"I'm sorry for your loss, Ruby."

Ruby's eyes shot up and for a moment she was taken back to the childhood she was just telling Ella about. Except the man standing before her wasn't a little boy anymore, he was a grown man.

"Jacob?" Ruby asked, completely flabbergasted.

A sad smile tugged at the corners of his mouth. "It's *gut* to see you, although the circumstances aren't."

Ruby shook her head. "How did you? Where do you? When…" she trailed off, not knowing what question to ask first. It had been such a long time since she saw Jacob walk out of the diner and she had thought about him a few times since then.

Jacob chuckled as he took a seat beside her beneath the tree. "Is there a question in there somewhere, or should I just start at the beginning?"

Ruby smiled. "That would be *gut*."

"After…after everything, I moved away. To this community, actually. I met a nice girl and finally realized that what we had, although it was special and built on friendship, was a childhood infatuation. I finally got over losing you to the baker," Jacob glanced at Ruby with a teasing grin, "and I fell in love. I'm married, Ruby."

"Jacob, I'm so happy for you. I'm so sorry for everything that happened."

Jacob nodded. "Me too. But at least I got to see Mary again before the accident. It was a few months ago, she'd just had Ella and we bumped into each other in town. She looked happy, radiant with it."

Ruby smiled before she sighed happily. "I'm glad to know she was happy. This little girl is going to miss out on knowing her parents and it just breaks my heart."

"But she'll have you to tell her all about the mischief we used to get up to." Jacob smiled.

Ruby laughed. "I think I'll pass on those memories. Ach Jacob, it's so *gut* to see you. To know she saw you before…"

"Hullo?"

Ruby glanced up at Daniel and smiled. In her arms, Ella was already reaching for Daniel to pick her up. Daniel took Ella while Ruby and Jacob stood up.

"Daniel Fischer, I'd like you to meet Jacob, my childhood friend."

Daniel's brows lifted, but he didn't miss a beat. "It's a pleasure to finally meet you, Jacob. I hope our *seeh* one day has the privilege of having such a *gut* friend."

At that moment Ruby wanted to kiss Daniel for his kindness. With his words, it was as if the past had finally moved into the background and the future lay before them with new hope. She glanced over at the graves and knew Mary would have been elated to see her and Jacob reconnect.

"Well, Ruby here was quite a spitfire. Always got me into trouble."

Ruby playfully swatted Jacob's arm. "Does your wife know you're prone to white lies?"

Jacob laughed. "*Nee*, but let's keep it a secret. It's *gut* to see you, Ruby."

"*Denke* for coming to today, Jacob."

Jacob nodded and glanced at Ella in David's arms. "I had to come and say goodbye. Whatever might have happened to us, we were once best friends. I know now that she never meant to hurt either of us, she just wanted to be loved."

Ruby wiped away a tear. "And she was loved. Caleb loved her more than anyone."

Daniel wrapped an arm around Ruby's shoulder. "Should we go get something to drink?"

Ruby summoned a smile as she glanced at her husband before meeting her childhood friend's gaze. "Let's do that and then we'll make a toast on Mary and all the *gut* times we shared."

Together they joined the other mourners, but Ruby couldn't help but be hopeful. Hopeful that the future would be better and that she would let Mary's little girl only remember her mother as the wonderful sister and wife she was.

# Epilogue

*Three years later...*

After a very long day at the bakery, Ruby couldn't wait to get home. Instead of taking the buggy, she left it for Daniel and decided to walk home. She got more than enough exercise constantly running after two toddlers, but she wanted the time to herself.

Today it had been three years since the day Mary died.

The first two years were hard. Especially when Ruby looked into Ella's eyes to see that they were the same color as Mary's. She would remember her sister and the pain would momentarily stun her until she regained her strength again. But the greatest gift Mary could have given her was Ella.

One day she would try explaining to both Ella and David that they were cousins, but for now she didn't stop them when they called each other *bruder and sissie*. The endearment was too beautiful to ruin with practicalities.

They had stayed in Lancaster for three weeks after

the funeral to make sure all Caleb and Mary's affairs were sorted before they returned to Ohio. Her parents, still struck down by their daughter's sudden death, had joined them in Ohio and had stayed with Elizabeth for the duration of their visit.

A month later they had returned to Lancaster to deal with their own affairs and were now happily living in the *dawdi haus* that Daniel had added to their home. It was the perfect arrangement. During the day while Daniel and Ruby worked, they had their grandchildren to tend to, and in the evenings they either visited with Elizabeth or the friends they had made since moving to Ohio.

Ruby often wondered if they would have moved had Mary survived, but she pushed that thought aside. She had learned a while ago that what-ifs brought nothing but pain and misery, and that it was best to remain focused on what was.

She had a beautiful family, a wonderful husband and two little bundles of joy that were now all of five and three years old.

The bond between her and Ella had been instant; from the first moment she had taken Ella in her arms, she had loved her as if she were her own. For Daniel, it had taken longer. But soon Ella had crawled into his heart just as she had crawled into Ruby's. Their life wouldn't be complete without Ella and her abundant giggles that reminded Ruby so much of Mary.

They were blessed and Ruby thanked God every single night for all the blessings in her life.

The sun was shining down on her as if God was blessing her with a lovely day as she walked home. In the distance she could see her father in the garden teaching David how to plant flowers while her mother sat on the porch braiding Ella's hair.

Ruby smiled up at the sky and closed her eyes even as she took a deep breath. "I can feel you watching over us, Mary. Keep watching."

She opened the garden gate and prepared herself for the bundle of energy that raced towards her in the form of little David. "*Mamm! Grossdaadi* just help me throw a flower."

"You mean he helped you sew a seed?" Ruby asked taking in a deep breath of sunshine, dirt and little boy. The smell was an amazing combination that she had come to love.

"*Jah*, and soon it's going to grow. Then we're going to pick it." He giggled as Ruby scooped him up and started towards the porch.

"Hullo *Mamm*, *Daed*," Ruby greeted her parents and set David down on the porch just as Ella spotted her.

Without even a thought for her *grossmammi* who was still busy with her hair, she jumped free and rushed to Ruby, *"Mamm!"*

In the beginning, she had tried to correct Ella whenever she called her *mamm*, until her own mother finally told her not to. Ella was simply doing what David was doing; it was no use trying to explain it to her now. Mary would always be Ella's mother, but so was Ruby. It was Ruby who soothed her hurts and who held her when she slept.

"Ella!" Ruby laughed with the same enthusiasm. "How was your day?"

"*Grossmammi* said I should learn how to braid my hair because it doesn't fit underneath my *kapp* otherwise."

Ruby looked down at the rough tumble of hair that was as abundant as Ella's smiles, and nodded. "No one makes a better braid that your *grossmammi*. Go on, let her finish."

"How was your day?" Ruby's mother asked when Ella repositioned herself on her lap once more.

"It was long, but it was *gut*. Daniel made the most interesting pastries today. He called them something French. Oh, that's right, a croissant. He puts chocolate inside before he bakes them, and they are simply heavenly."

"That sounds *gut*. And your cake, did you manage to finish it?"

Ruby nodded. She had stopped baking from home about a year ago when she realized that between David and Ella there wasn't going to be any frosting left to put on the cake once they knew there was frosting in the kitchen. "*Jah*, it turned out nicely."

"I'm sure they're going to be very happy," her mother assured her. Ruby's Wedding Cakes were the latest addition to Ruby's bakery. Apparently her rates were much more affordable than the other vendors in town and there was no doubt that they tasted much better.

"I hope so. Are you staying for dinner?" Ruby asked as she did most nights.

Her mother shook her head. "*Nee*, we'll give you some time with your *familye*. Your *daed* and I were thinking of taking a walk down to the river."

Ruby's eyes widened. "That's quite a long walk."

"Exactly, gets the juices pumping again. Come along, David."

Both her father and her son rushed to her mother's

side, making Ruby laugh. "Not you, you're staying right here with me. Want to help me cook?"

David and Ella nodded eagerly, taking Ruby's hand as her parents left through the garden gate. This was her favorite time of day, when she had a couple of hours just to spend with the children. It was the time of day when she knew how blessed she was to have been asked to be Ella's guardian. Together they walked into the kitchen and started dinner.

Ruby had long since stopped complaining about the mess they made whenever they tried to help, instead she let them be. If she had learned anything from losing her sister, it was that life was too short to fight over the inconsequential in the long run. By the time Daniel arrived, the stew was almost done, and the kitchen just about remedied after the onslaught of the toddlers.

"That smells amazing," Daniel said as he walked through the door.

Ruby laughed, shaking her head as she dusted flour off her apron. "I hope it tastes amazing. There might be a few ingredients in there that were strategically placed by David and Ella."

"At least they're helping," Daniel laughed.

"You're right, at least they're helping." Ruby smiled. "How was the rest of the afternoon?"

"Great. The couple were very happy with the cake. They kept going on and on about how talented you are."

"That's *gut* to hear; at least I know you won't forget it any time soon."

Daniel smiled and stepped closer, pulling Ruby into his arms. "How can I ever forget what a *gut* person you are? Just look at this kitchen."

They both glanced around at the eggshells on the floor yet to be picked up and the flour on the table.

"Any other mother would have chastened them, but you let them play, you let them be happy. You are a blessing to us, Ruby."

"You are my blessing, Daniel. Have I told you today how much I love you?"

Daniel shrugged, "Maybe, briefly, but I'd be happy to hear it again."

"I love you, Daniel; I'd love you more if you help me clean the kitchen."

Daniel laughed and quickly jumped back. "I'll give the *kinners* their bath, that way you can love me even more because they're out of your hair while you're cleaning up."

Ruby laughed as he disappeared into the hallway. For a while their lives had been filled with sadness and loss but somehow through prayer and family, they had found their joy again. They had found a way to celebrate Mary and Caleb's lives instead of mourning their death.

Somehow, Ruby thought as she wiped flour off her cheek, she had struck gold when she met Daniel.

Children's laughter sounded through the house as she picked up the eggshells and, instead of being mad, she prayed that tomorrow she would get to do it all over again.

\* \* \* \* \*